The TRUST Charm
A Finding Faith Romance

Jessica Alyse

Published 2015

ISBN: 978-0-692-56933-7

Bluebonnets and Barbed Wire Publishing House®

All rights reserved. No part of this book may be reproduced in any form, except for brief quotations in printed reviews, without permission in writing from the publisher.

Edited by Lesley Ann McDaniel

ACKNOWLEDGMENTS

First, to my family whose support brought me through it all, from endless ideas and horrible rough drafts to my first book. I love you Mom, Dad, Tiffany, and Mike.

To my cousin, the Sister of my Creativity, Samantha Craft, for being my constant over the years. When I was flooded with fear you showed me courage. When I was discouraged you taught me patience.

To Avon Knowlton and Ruth Wells for unconditional encouragement. You believed in me before you really knew me and your hopes never faded. I'm humbled by your unwavering kindness.

To Penny Zeller, for being the first author to listen to this young girl's crazy dreams about writing. Thank you, Penny.

To my beta readers, Liddia Rougeou, Reagan Craig, and Chelsea Welch. And to my editor, Lesley Ann McDaniel. Thank you guys so much.

To those who helped me with the research for this book. Stefanie Nelson and Crystal Klyng, my go-to girls for anything Houston. Donna Marshall Yates and Brittany Pfantz, who helped make my first chapter perfect. Gloria Gentry, who fined tuned the law enforcement details. Destin Singletary, who has used her dreams to help me accomplish mine by overseeing the hospital scenes.

And last but certainly not least, to JoAnn Durgin, Bonnie S. Calhoun, and the Christian Indie Authors Group. Without your knowledge and willingness to reach out to a new author, self-publishing wouldn't have been possible for me.

Thank you all.

DEDICATION

This book is dedicated to my Lord and Savior,
Jesus Christ. For without His grace I would have no
purpose. My King and Strong Tower, I have loved nothing
more than I have loved You. It's because of Your cross
that I know what love really looks like.

The TRUST Charm

CHAPTER ONE

Avery Sanders vowed to never love a man like him.

He wore tan and brown fatigues with an embroidered patch that read *Callahan*. A hometown hero, he earned her deepest respect. But she couldn't see past a man whose life was no longer than the barrel of his gun. Pity the young woman sitting across the table from him and the babe she cradled in her arms.

"Avery?" Carol Ellert, Avery's younger sister, stood on the other side of the pastry counter.

Avery slipped back into work mode and grabbed a porcelain cup half-filled with espresso. "What?"

"Are you listening to me?"

"Sure." She tucked a strand of dark-brown hair behind her ear and poured foam over the espresso. "But say it again so I know we're on the same page."

Carol exhaled impatiently. "Please, come sit down while you're still on your break."

Avery topped off the latté with a drizzle of caramel syrup. "Here's your—"

Carol was gone. Across the café she eased into a chair with the help of her husband, Branson, while keeping her hand on her pregnant midsection.

Avery went to her table and set the cup in front of her. "Coffee's bad for the baby."

"He'll enjoy it. Have a sit."

Avery sat and crossed one leg over the other. Her bracelet brushed the aluminum tabletop. She grabbed the longest charm, the one that read "trust" and rubbed her fingers against the sleek surface, a habit she'd picked up eight years ago when she'd gotten the bracelet as a Christmas present from their parents. "What's up?"

"We're moving."

It'd been a long time coming but it still felt like a baseball bat to the gut. "What did you decide on? Jersey or Queens?"

"Actually...Italy."

Avery dropped the charm. "Italy? Are you kidding?"

From Carol's scrunched nose to Branson's wrinkled forehead, she figured they weren't. "Where did Italy come from? I thought you needed to be in New York for Branson's job?"

"Our options are New York and Rome." Branson propped his arm behind Carol and cupped her shoulder. "We always talked about living in a different country."

"But it was only a dream we shared. We never thought it could be a possibility."

Avery picked up Carol's coffee. "It's longer than a four-hour flight, but hey, as long as you're happy."

"I think we will be." Carol dropped her hand on Branson's knee.

"When do you leave?" Avery took a sip.

"Three weeks after the baby's born. Three months from now if he's on time." She rubbed her belly. "We're going to fly to Alabama and visit with Mom and Dad for a couple days. Then Branson's company wants him there ASAP."

"That soon, huh? I won't even get a chance to teach Junior how to mix a cup of joe."

Carol tucked her short, bobbed cut behind one ear.

"It's funny you say that. We were hoping you'd want to come with us."

Avery coughed into the coffee. Warm drops ran down her fingers.

Carol's eyes widened. "I'm not going to want that back."

"You're not serious." Avery set the cup down and wiped her hand against her apron. "You want me to go with you? Like, live with you? In Rome?"

"Plane tickets aren't entirely impossible. And I was hoping you wouldn't mind taking a job as our nanny."

Branson shifted. "I'd feel better being at work if someone were at the house helping Carol. And she mentioned that you've always wanted to study coffee abroad."

Avery imagined the posters of giant coffee beans hanging on her childhood bedroom walls, luring the depths of her soul; *Venha e aproveite com a gente Brasil*, beckoning her to come and enjoy Brazil.

Okay, so Rome was no Brazil.

But it would do.

"Yes. If you're sure you want me. Of course I'll go. I need to talk to Grace."

Grace. Their oldest sister and Avery's roommate of five years.

"I'm sure Grace would be happy for you. We can all meet up after you get off work and tell her together?"

Across the room, glass crashed against the tiled floor.

The soldier knelt down on bended knee picking up pieces of white porcelain from a puddle of coffee.

"I'll be right back." Avery left her sister and stepped behind the counter for the broom and dustpan.

"Let me, sir." She gave him a smile. He dropped the broken pieces in her dustpan and took his seat.

The soldier's wife sniffled. Avery opened her mouth to say the cup could be replaced when she heard the young woman plead, "I don't want you to leave again."

Avery froze, hands curled around the handle, head bowed. The soldier hesitated, and then said with confidence, "It's my job, Carrie. I have to go."

The girl began to cry. The baby wailed against her shoulder. Sadness thickened the air around Avery. Or was that the lump in her throat? It may have been the heavy clouds hanging above the coffee shop, threatening to cry with the soldier's wife. Unsure of which, Avery walked around the bar and shouldered through the swinging door.

But one thing she was sure of.

She vowed to never love a man like him.

Shopping on Valentine's Day had always been a nightmare for a single girl like Avery.

The most romantic, witty, and attractive men gathered for the country's largest ineligible bachelor convention.

Or so it seemed.

Bernfeld's shelves were stocked floor to ceiling with roses, curve-hugging chocolate, and sappy cards that could prompt a squeal and guarantee a kiss from even the most pessimistic sweetheart. It was tough enough to go it alone, chocolate-less and gift-barren, but then Avery had to brave the aisles of men who'd forgotten how special today was until the last minute. They were quick to shoot a smile her way while holding a dozen roses and an oversized stuffed puppy.

Grace had requested a gallon of laundry detergent and Avery obliged. If it were up to her, Avery would have forsaken the detergent until tomorrow. Now, all she wanted was to get back to Midtown.

Detergent in hand, she aimed her sights on the checkout counter and walked past a guy whose cologne grabbed her attention. It was easy not taking a second look. The hard part was wondering if she'd ever bumped into her future husband here buying a gift for his current girlfriend. Harder still were the occasional nights she lay awake considering that, at twenty-nine, there might not be a future husband for her.

On the other hand, the candy aisle knew how to appease a woman. What could a few extra pounds in self-pity do to her hips in one day?

Avery changed directions and planned a new route. One bag of chocolate and caramel-covered cashews. Grace would thank her later.

Just her luck—nothing but an empty cardboard box awaited her. "You've got to be kidding me."

"Bernfeld's would make more commission if they kept their shelves stocked," said some guy to her right.

A bit taller than her and broad in the shoulders, his gray T-shirt fit him well. He gave her a smirk, complete with stubble-covered dimples. His eyes were blue with a dark brown blemish on the upper half of his right iris.

She might consider him attractive if he weren't holding a box of candy in the shape of a heart. There was something unappealing about another girl's boyfriend.

"Now that would be the smart move."

"For some reason we keep coming back, expecting something different." He picked up a box, listened to the sound of broken cookies, and laid it back on the shelf.

"I think they call that insanity."

He smiled her way again, a bit less reserved. "Can I ask your opinion?"

She fought back a sigh. "Why not?"

"What should I get a woman who doesn't like chocolate?"

"Is this your first date with her?"

His dark eyebrows furrowed. "Not exactly."

"If you're buying candy for a woman you consider a valentine, you should probably know her well enough to know what she likes."

"You've got a point." He turned toward her.

"I'll give you advice but if you strike out, it's on you."

"I'm willing to take the risk."

Avery switched the detergent to her other hand and gestured to a box of gummy candy. "If she's funny and spirited then she'll probably like some kind of taffy or something sour. If she's serious and to herself then she'll probably like a bucket of mints or butterscotch. If she reads books then you'll want to opt for a gift card to her favorite coffee shop. She'll fall in love with you on the spot. Whatever the case, you can always use a dozen roses to overshadow the candy."

She could tell from his sober eyes that she had his undivided attention.

"I guess I asked the right person."

"Well, there is that whole 'I'm a girl' thing."

"All right. What about this?" He picked up an out-of-place bottle of cheap wine.

"If you don't know the girl very well then she may misinterpret what you're giving her." She put a hand up. "Unless you're that kind of guy."

"I'm not." He shook his head and replaced the bottle. "So what did you get for Valentine's?"

"Laundry detergent. Can't beat a pair of fresh pants." That was weird. She resisted the urge to smack her head.

"I'm sure your boyfriend will appreciate that."

"I don't have a—ah." Avery nodded with a grin. "That's one way of asking if I'm single."

"You caught that, did you?" He lowered his head.

She started to back away. "In that case I'll be straightforward with you. I'm not interested in guys who already have girlfriends."

"Who said I have a girlfriend?"

"Seriously?" She sarcastically dropped her attention to the box in his hand. "This place is crawling with unavailable men. You're holding a huge, red heart. And you asked me what kind of candy you should buy a girl. It's kind of evident at this point."

"You assumed I was seeing someone. I never said I was."

She thought back on his first question. Had she misunderstood? What was this conversation about again?

"I'm buying candy for a friend of mine. She happens to be a grandmother. Like you, I'm very single."

Did he have to use the word "very"?

"But if you give me your number we could change that."

Oh, he was good. This guy was double dipped in charm. Fighting back a grin, Avery took a closer look at him.

Subtly charismatic with long dimples, skin a lighter shade than her Latin-American tan, and short, styled coffee-brown hair. She wouldn't mind letting this guy take her out.

"That *would* change things, wouldn't it?" she said while Italian-accented voices at the back of her thoughts warned her not to lose sight of the fact that she would be leaving the country in a few months. Bummer. "I can't. Sorry. I don't give out my number."

"But what if I never see you again?" Somehow he made it sound tragic.

Avery's shoulders fell. "Do you believe in fate?"

"I believe in God."

She stopped. "Then we'll leave it up to Him. If we're meant to meet again, we will."

"And you'll let me take you out?" He gave her a half-smile.

How likely was it that, in all of Houston, she'd run into him again? "Sure, why not."

She turned and walked away, confident she'd never see this guy again.

Just her luck.

CHAPTER TWO

Sky-high businesses, fresh air laced with energy, and the constant rhythm of Houston traffic, Liam Reed wouldn't have it any other way. His heart lived here alongside his badge.

"Three eighty-five. We have a possible break-in."

Liam pressed the radio on his shoulder. "Copy."

The dispatcher rattled off the address of an abandoned house on Wheeler Avenue.

"Ten four," Liam relayed and flipped on his blinker.

He scanned the rearview mirror and caught a glimpse of his right eye where dark brown marked the upper half of the blue iris. An imperfection that had claimed him since birth.

When traffic was clear he turned onto Wheeler Avenue. "I was thinking it's been a while since we've seen a burglary."

Austin Brooks, Liam's partner of four years, lounged in his seat. "I was thinking about lunch."

Austin had a dry sense of humor that could be appreciated when the time was right. But the twenty-three year old didn't have the best timing. Some days he leaned more on the immature side. Liam could probably blame that on the kid's upbringing, but all Liam knew was that he'd had it hard growing up and nearly lost it all in the process.

When the two-story house came into view, Austin sat upright. Liam surveyed broken windows and gutters hanging haphazardly from the roof as he parallel parked on the street. They left the cruiser and walked across an overgrown lawn. The withered boards on the porch whined under their weight. A piece of plywood that covered the entryway had been pried back.

Liam wrestled the plywood away from the doorway and set it aside.

Austin leaned into the living room. "Police. Show yourself."

Not a sound. Nor a sign of life. The place had been ransacked ten times over and what thieves hadn't taken now littered the floor. The room felt like it sat on the surface of the sun and the smell of mold hung unbearably thick around them.

Something faint shuffled in the back room, light enough for Liam to write it off as a rat.

"Show yourself," Liam repeated.

Footfalls drummed against the stairway on the other side of the wall. Liam glanced at Austin. Austin focused on the ceiling.

They rushed through the living room, stumbling over trash and wrecked furniture. After a scan to confirm the kitchen was empty Liam took the stairs first, drawing his gun but keeping it aimed at the floor.

He moved swiftly, his back against the wall. The beat of his heart reverberated through his chest. Sweat collected on his collar.

"Come on, guy. Show yourself and we can keep the peace, here." Liam's mind raced with scenarios.

Gunfire. Shadows. Someone hiding behind him. A chill crept up his spine, forcing him to spare a look downstairs, past Austin, into the darkness. But he found nobody.

Above him, a door squealed on tired hinges. Hair on the back of his neck rose.

The window at the top of the stairs gradually came into view. Four rooms. Two on each side. Liam peered in the right. Empty. Austin looked into the opposite room and shook his head.

They continued to the next two rooms. Liam moved slowly until he could see a closet door.

"Psst." Austin drew Liam's attention to the opposite room. "Cover me."

Liam turned his back to the window where he had his sights set on both rooms and the hallway.

Austin progressed cautiously until he was in front of the closet. He twisted the knob slowly and the muscles in Liam's shoulders tensed as he prepared for what might come. Austin threw the door open.

Dust drifted across the rays of sun streaming between Liam and Austin. The closet was empty, except a few wire hangers.

Liam stepped into the last room and moved toward the closet.

"Show us your hands," Austin called out.

Gun ready, Liam's breaths grew heavy in his chest. The floor creaked beneath his shoes. Dust drifted from the gap at the bottom of the door. Ears ringing from the silence, he reached for the knob. It felt cold in his hand, its twist stubborn.

When he cleared the kink, he swung the door open and leveled his aim.

Inside sat a boy with his arms around his knees, peering up at Liam with wide eyes.

Liam exhaled and lowered his gun. "Justin Jacobs." He swiped his sleeve across the sweat on his forehead. "Is there anyone else in the house?"

JJ shook his head.

Liam holstered his weapon and glanced at Austin. "What's the story, JJ?"

The kid shrugged and chewed on his bottom lip.

"Come on out of there."

JJ pulled himself up. "I was just lookin'."

"It's called breaking and entering, JJ," Austin said from the doorway. "It's a crime."

JJ's jaw quivered as he swallowed, but his brave façade remained intact.

"Take anything?"

"No." He didn't have any pockets on his sweats and his T-shirt hung against his small ribcage.

"All right. Let's go."

Liam led JJ out of the house and across the lawn. He opened the back door of the cruiser and JJ slid in out of habit.

Liam got behind the wheel. "JJ, where's your dad?"

In the rearview mirror, the boy's shoulders lifted and fell. "Ain't seen him in a month."

It was a crying shame. Liam had dealt with Charlie Jacobs in the past, a man who had a knack for trouble, and his son followed closely in his footsteps.

A five minute drive brought Liam to a mint green house in need of new shutters. He opened the door and JJ trudged up the walkway, past his grandmother. She pulled him against her for a quick hug before he carried himself over the threshold.

Dorinda Jacobs set a hand against the porch post. "Thank you, officers."

"It's not a problem."

She shook her head, lips pursed. "What's he done now?"

"Nothing much." Austin shrugged and ran his fingers through his hair. "He did an unauthorized investigation of an abandoned house on Wheeler Avenue. No worries. He was just giving us a hand."

"I'll talk to him," she said.

She did that every day. Liam knew. But it didn't work. Without a dad in the picture, no grandfather, and a grandmother who worked overtime at the hospital in the medical center, JJ had no outlet for the anger that had built up since his mom's death. Which was why Liam made a habit of taking him to the youth center on his days off. Socializing helped, but it wasn't enough.

"I didn't even know he left the house." Dorinda sighed. "Must have slipped out the window. I'll try to get a better eye on him. I keep trying…"

"You're doing a fine job, Dorinda. He's at a tough age. He'll get through it. So will you." Liam hooked his thumbs behind his gun belt.

She nodded with a wrinkle between her brows. "Maybe I've learned from my mistakes by now."

"We live and learn," Austin mumbled.

"You call us if you need us." Liam nodded and went to get into the cruiser.

"Liam?" Dorinda called out.

Liam stopped short and looked at her over the roof. "Ma'am?"

"Just so you know, I wasn't here on Valentine's Day, but I found them butterscotch candies you left on my table. And I know it was you who left 'em there, can't pull the wool over my eyes, Officer Reed. Anyhow, they're my favorite. It was very kind of you."

"I'm glad you liked them." He bit back a smile and shook his head, remembering a certain tan-skinned beauty with a gallon of laundry detergent. "Someone told me you'd like them."

CHAPTER THREE

Avery had waited weeks for this. Six weeks, to be exact, since she'd applied for a volunteer position at the Consumed Youth Community Center. Long before she made plans to leave Houston for Rome.

Now, with the understanding that this wasn't a long-term commitment, she followed the director down the whitewashed hallway that smelled like bleach and glue.

"I apologize beforehand." Kellie Swanson stopped in front of a set of double doors.

"For?"

She jerked her head toward a big sign that read *Gym*. "You'll have to go through here to get to the auditorium."

"I don't mind."

Kellie gave her a doubtful shrug and propelled the door open.

Avery wasn't afraid of a little sweat and—

The thunder of basketballs and screech of sneakers drowned out her thoughts. There were kids everywhere. Little kids, big kids. Laughing, screaming, running like their lives depended on it. Oh, to have that kind of energy again.

Kellie raised her voice. "Your students will be quieter than this."

"We can only—" Avery stopped short. Her heart skipped a beat and the sound of screaming kids faded away.

It was him. Across the gym was the man she'd met at Bernfeld's. The one she never thought she'd see again. He was dressed in shorts and a Longhorns T-shirt, besting a teen his size at a game of one-on-one.

"I can't believe it," she mumbled.

The basketball bounced down the sideline and he went after it, stopping right in front of Kellie, who slowed her pace.

He looked up at Avery and his eyes went wide. "Hi."

Avery smiled. Apparently the odds were in her favor after all. "Hi."

"You know each other?" Kellie glanced between the two of them as Avery approached.

"We've met. Informally."

"Over a bottle of wine on Valentine's Day," he said, wearing a grin.

"That's way out of context." Avery's heart leapt into her throat. She couldn't believe he just said that. But she wouldn't deny the humor behind it.

Kellie's eyebrows disappeared behind her gray bangs.

The gym got quieter as a large group of kids exited out the side door, leaving behind a few stragglers.

He reached out to shake her hand. "Liam Reed."

"Avery Sanders."

"Avery." He repeated softly, his voice low and deep.

"Avery is our newest volunteer." Kellie touched her shoulder. "She'll be working with our theatre students."

"Yeah?" He grinned, showing those dimples. "I could take her to the auditorium."

"That would be great. Thank you." She turned to Avery. "If you need anything, you know where to find me." She backed away with a smile and left through the double doors.

Avery fell in line beside Liam. His leisure pace didn't go

unnoticed. Was he working up the nerve to ask her out or would he take his time getting to know her first? Either way, she was excited.

She shrugged her purse further up her shoulder. "So you're stalking me, now?"

He opened his mouth but hesitated. "I've been working here for ten years so I guess I should ask you the same thing."

"Touché." She gave him a sidelong glance.

The only thing different about him was his hair. Damp with perspiration, it laid against his forehead in short, nearly black tufts. He looked her way and she noticed the blemish on his right eye.

An abandoned ball rolled into their path. He spun it back and kicked it up into his reach.

"So you're a coach?"

"Unelected, I guess you could say. I help out where I can but I like to stay close to sports."

She was sure he did. With shoulders like that he was undeniably cut out for it. She cleared her throat.

"You didn't think we would meet again, did you?" He bounced the ball.

"Did you?" Why was it so warm all of a sudden?

He gave a halfhearted attempt to shoot toward a goal too far away. "The thought crossed my mind once or twice."

She stopped in front of the exit, her hand trembled against the latch. "So what does this mean?"

He looked like he was holding back a grin. Could she blame him?

"I'm not going to ask you on a date."

What?

This guy got a second look at her and decided she wasn't his type?

Or maybe he'd been throwing her a bone when he'd asked her out. Or maybe he'd met someone else since that day.

Whatever the case, she felt like she'd just been slapped.

"Okay." She forced a smile. No hard feelings.

What did it matter anyway? She was leaving the country and any potential relationships would only make things complicated.

She pushed the latch and prayed these doors led to the auditorium. Instead, she found herself standing on a concrete walkway outside. What looked like the entrance was a short ways across from her. Her heartbeat banged against her chest so loudly she was sure he could hear it.

"Is this it?" She dipped her head toward the next set of doors.

"I didn't mean that like it sounded." He stayed on her heels.

She would take that as a yes.

"It's not that I *don't* want to go out with you."

Now would be a great time for her to give her two weeks' notice.

He grabbed the door handle for her but didn't open it. "What I meant was I would never force a woman to go out with me."

That sober look in his hooded eyes was an apology. But it didn't help the humiliation she felt seeping into her soul.

"I get it. Really. Don't worry about it."

His smirk told her he wasn't convinced.

Was she being transparent? Avery resisted the urge to roll her eyes. "I didn't mean to take offense. It's just that it sounded like—"

"Like you weren't worth a second look."

Wow. "Thanks for putting it into words."

His smile turned into a grimace. "This is a horrible first impression, isn't it?"

"No." She shook her head. "Your first impression was on the money. It's the second impression we're stumbling over."

"I'm going to leave you to it now. Just promise you won't hold it against me." He started to pull the door open.

She pushed her hand flush against it and closed her eyes.

This was silly.

But she would say it anyway. "Hey. I know you. We met on Valentine's Day. Remember? Over a *bottle of wine*." She winked.

Avery took pleasure in the slow grin that crawled across his face. "Yeah…yeah, I remember. It's hard to forget a pretty face."

She offered him her hand. "Avery Sanders."

"Liam Reed."

"I look forward to working with you, Liam."

"And I look forward to getting to know you." He swung the door open.

She walked inside and kept her focus on the stage at the other end of the aisle, her tongue tied in knots and dry against the roof her mouth. If she turned back now, she might be the one to say something redundant and ruin a second impression.

CHAPTER FOUR

For the fifth evening in two weeks Avery tried to walk through the gym without noticing Liam.

She failed miserably. He'd even caught her looking once or twice. And each time she wanted to throw herself through the emergency exit at the side of the gym.

There was just something commandeering about him. Authoritative. Trustworthy.

She lost the battle with her curiosity and looked his way. He stood beside a kid, basketball in hands, showing him how to shoot.

Avery returned her focus on the auditorium when she came across a small boy sitting against the wall on the sidelines. Shoulders slumped, arms wrapped around his shins, he seemed in dire need of some encouragement.

She glanced at the time on her phone and found a few minutes to spare.

"Hi, I'm Avery."

He peeked up at her, his thin eyebrows upturned. "JJ."

"You don't play basketball?"

"I'm too small."

There were a lot of kids on the court. Boys and girls, big and small alike.

She crouched down beside him. "Well, I was always told to never let anything get in the way of what I love."

He shifted around and propped his chin on his arm. "You like basketball?"

"It's all right. Do you?"

He hesitated then shrugged.

"I've got a feeling you do."

"A little," he said quickly.

"For what it's worth, JJ, I don't think you're too small. I think you're more than capable of getting out there and making some baskets." Or whatever they're called.

A smirk flashed behind his veil of shyness so quickly that she wondered if she only imagined it. That was a shame.

She looked up and found Liam across the court, watching her. Her breath hitched in her chest. He lifted his hand and she waved back.

JJ shoved himself off the ground and jogged onto the court.

Avery stood and continued toward the exit. She checked the time again and heard someone call her name.

Liam.

She turned around.

"I can't believe you got him to play."

"JJ?" she asked. The boy was across the court in a group of kids closer to his size. "That was all him. I was just trying to make small talk."

"I've been trying to get that kid to socialize for almost a year now and nada. And then you come along."

"I'm sorry, I didn't mean to interfere with anything."

"Don't apologize." Liam shook his head. "You did in five minutes what I couldn't do in six months. I'm impressed. And uh…somewhat smitten."

Heat flooded up her neck. "That's just a temporary side effect. It'll go away once you get to know me better."

He chuckled. She didn't mind seeing those dimples again.

She held his blue-eyed gaze as he backed away. When he turned toward the court she slipped outside. The warm Texas air hit her, yet she shivered. That man made her weak at the knees.

The door broke open behind her and light spilled over the sidewalk. "Wait."

He stuck his hands into his pockets. "I was wondering," he paused long enough to moisten his lips. "Would it be too soon if I asked you out?"

"Too soon?"

His smile turned into a grin and he bounced forward on his tiptoes. "I didn't want to seem presumptuous."

She chewed on her bottom lip and lifted her shoulders. "I can't say I didn't exactly see this coming."

"What do you say? Pick you up Friday at seven?"

Avery felt her smile slip away. Carol and Branson were coming over Friday night. Carol planned to bring pamphlets about Italy and pictures of the house they wanted to buy.

Italy. And then there was that.

How could one city ruin a girl's night?

Avery's phone buzzed against her palm and Grace's name flashed across the notification bar along with a text. Something about picking up cokes on her way home. Avery turned off the screen and shook her head.

"I can't. I have plans." Big plans.

She started to back away, wishing she didn't have to.

"Those plans don't overlap into Saturday, do they?"

She couldn't help but smile. "Technically, no. They don't."

"Would you like to have dinner with me on Saturday?"

She had a choice to make. Put Italy on the back burner and take a gamble on where this might lead. Or start over in a new, exciting city and risk walking away from true love.

True love?

Avery looked into Liam's eyes.

Could she see herself with this man? Could she imagine sharing a life with him? A mentor to youth. A person who buys Valentine's gifts for grandmothers. A man who claims God over fate. Did she want to take a chance on finding true love with Liam Reed?

"Yes." She was already loosing herself to the thought of him. "I would love to have dinner with you on Saturday."

CHAPTER FIVE

Liam scanned the apartment number and let himself exhale one last time as he knocked on her door. He started to shove his hands in his pockets but thought twice about it. The moisture on his palms drove him insane. Of all the annoying traits, why this—

The door swung open and a short, balding man looked Liam up and down through round-rimmed glasses. "Can I help you?"

"Um…" Not the stunning female he'd been expecting. "Is Avery here?"

The plump man blinked twice and pointed down the hall.

"Of course." Liam's shoulders fell. "Sorry 'bout that. Have a nice night."

He nodded and closed the door.

Liam looked around for witnesses, debating whether or not to abandon the night. He pulled Avery's directions from his pocket and double checked the apartment number. Three eleven. The numbers were written clearly but somehow he found himself standing in front of three ten instead. "I'm an idiot."

He tucked the paper back in his pocket and kicked the

carpet as he made his way to Avery's apartment. He knocked, hoping this was the right door.

Avery appeared on the other side and made him lose all train of thought. Seeing her dressed in a forest green blouse that looked amazing with her skin tone, and a black skirt that reached her knees, he found it hard to speak. Her cheeks were rosy, a lot rosier than the last time he saw her. As were her lips.

"Wow." He cleared his throat. "You look beautiful."

She stepped toward him and closed the door behind her. "Thank you. You look very handsome."

He stayed near her side as they walked down the hall and into the stairwell. His heartbeat had wandered into his throat.

"I'm sorry I couldn't introduce you to my sister. She's actually on call for an emergency surgery," she said.

"She's a doctor?"

"Vet, actually."

"That's cool. If my goldfish ever gets sick I'll be sure to give her a call." What was he thinking? He wanted to slam his head against the wall.

"Oh, you—you have a goldfish?"

"No. I don't. I was kidding."

She gave him a look from the corner of her eyes that said she didn't entirely believe him.

Outside, Liam opened the truck door for her. He couldn't help but notice the way her hand so naturally slipped into his as she slid inside.

He shut the door behind her and got into the driver's side. "Do you like Italian?"

She jerked her focus to him, her mouth agape. Her hands tightened around her seatbelt. It seemed like she were waiting for him to tell her it was a joke.

"I love Italian."

This was a good start. "I take it you've been to Bella Lorenzo's."

"Of course. That's a great place."

He braved a look at her and was rewarded with that ready smile. She was like a breath of fresh air with her quick-as-a-whip charm and femininity. She tucked her straight hair, cut at a long angle on one side, behind her ear, giving him a clear view of her profile, her gorgeous eyes, long lashes, and soft lips.

He pulled out onto the road with a feeling of certainty banging against his chest.

"You've already told me about your sister. Is it just the two of you?" He pulled to a stop at a red light.

"I have two sisters. Grace is older. I moved in with her after her husband passed away. Carol is two years younger than me. She lives on the other side of Houston with her husband, Branson. They're expecting their first kid in a couple months."

"That's great."

"Do you have any siblings?"

"Only child." Practically an orphan after his mother left.

"I used to wish I was an only child." Avery lifted her shoulders. "All the time."

"What about now?"

She sighed. "I think when you grow up you make peace with life. I love my sisters. I wouldn't trade them for anything..."

He heard something hiding under her voice. "But?"

"Sometimes I just want to be my own person and stop living in their shadow."

"How's that?"

She hesitated. "Their lives are all but made for them. They went to college. Married young. Grace has her own clinic. Carol is a real estate broker, and she'll be a mom, soon. While I struggled through college, couldn't find a job..."

"And you're still single." Why did he say that out loud? What was he thinking? Liam looked out his window and shook his head.

"I didn't want say it out loud and risk sounding desperate, but yes. Thank you."

In a few minutes they were at the restaurant. He escorted her inside and they followed the hostess to a table lined with a pristine white cloth, crystal glasses turned upside down, and the dancing flame of a candle between them. Liam pulled out a chair.

"Thank you." Avery tucked her skirt beneath her. "Would you mind if I asked you a personal question—something I've been wondering about for a few days?"

He settled into the chair across from her and moistened his lips. "Uh, sure."

"How old are you?"

Liam couldn't help but chuckle. Not that he had anything to hide, but when someone says they have a personal question, his age wasn't what he would expect. "I'm thirty-two."

Her shoulders eased. "I've been trying to figure it out." She tilted her hand back and forth. "You look very young. I was hoping you weren't much younger than me."

Liam wanted to ask her age but a warning signal in his mind told him to avoid questions certain questions. How old are you? What size do you wear? How much do you weigh? Things like that.

She dipped her head and caught his focus. "In case you're wondering. I'm twenty-nine."

He exhaled. "I was."

When her laugh mingled with his, some of the tension disappeared from his chest.

By the time the food was served, Liam had learned that Avery was human. She was nervous, imperfect, and unabashedly blatant when it came to her wit.

"Thank you," he said to the server who set a plate in front of him.

This part of the date usually made him hesitant. But he hadn't abandoned his beliefs yet and he didn't plan on it tonight.

He'd encountered a few women—even self-proclaimed Christian women—who didn't care for a second date when Liam bowed his head to pray over dinner. There was something embarrassing, or maybe uncomfortable, about praying out loud. "Would you mind—"

"—Do you think—"

"I'm sorry." He tilted his head toward her. "Go ahead."

Her fingers fiddled with something on her bracelet. "Do you think it would be all right if we said grace?"

His heart raced. Her eyes were pinned on him, awaiting an answer. But he couldn't give one.

There were some things a man just knew. When he could call himself a man. When it was time to finish a fight. When a person couldn't be trusted. And when he was looking at his wife.

"Of course."

He watched her bow her head and he thought nothing looked as beautiful as Avery did in that moment. He closed his eyes and thanked God.

Over the course of the meal he learned a lot about her. Learned about her love for traveling, but her greater love for Houston. He learned that she was baptized at a young age, had slipped away in her teen years, and returned to the Lord in her early twenties. He learned that she was left-handed, she didn't like pets, and she smiled with her eyes when she was being witty and smiled with her mouth when *he* was being witty.

And it didn't take much to make her smile. He wondered if it was just him or if she was like that with everyone. As of yet, he wanted to believe it was only for him.

By the end of the night, they were in the truck nearing her apartment when Liam found the conversation had somehow returned to the subject of marriage. Funny how that kept coming up.

The bright lights of Midtown reflected on her face as they drove through the district.

"So you've never been married?" he asked.

"Not yet. I think it might have to do with my unconventional beliefs."

"Yeah?"

"Sure. I mean, there are certain guys I won't date, like servicemen. So that eliminates a lot of potentials."

Was he missing something? "What do you mean by servicemen?"

"Soldiers, cops, firemen...miners," she said with a laugh. "Guys who don't exactly have a job that guarantees tomorrow."

For a second, Liam thought he was dreaming. "You don't say."

"Yeah, I've never understood how men like that could get married. Why would you want to risk losing your life and make a family pay for it?"

He swallowed but the thrumming in his neck wouldn't go away. "What—what led you to these, uh, unconventional beliefs?"

"Just the kind of guys I've met in the past."

Liam wasn't sure if he wanted to pull over or drive faster. Either way, he needed to process this. She had to be joking. Maybe she knew he was a cop and she was teasing him.

"So what if, uh, you fell in love with a guy like that—a cop or fireman or something—you would break off the relationship?"

"It wouldn't be fair to lead him on. I couldn't have a future with a man like that."

Oh, boy. She was serious.

The woman of his dreams was sitting beside him, alluring him with thoughts of a future together, and she tells him that she'd walk away if she knew he was a cop.

This wasn't happening.

Lord, what was he supposed to say?

"Speaking of careers," she said.

A bead of sweat dripped down beneath his coat collar.

This was it. This was the end. He wouldn't even make it to a second date alive.

"Do you plan to work at the youth center for long?"

The ringing in his ears drowned out the car that honked behind him. The light was green. Liam hit the gas.

She thought he worked professionally at the center?

Against his better judgment Liam said the first thing that came to mind.

CHAPTER SIX

"For as long as I can." Liam told Austin the next morning, after a sleepless night.

"Whoa. So you're telling me this girl thinks you work at the center full-time?" Austin sounded as surprised as Liam had felt seven hours ago.

"Yep."

"And she'd break up with you if she knew you were a cop?"

Liam turned into the dim parking lot of a twenty-four hour diner. He needed coffee.

"Sounds like a Christian if I ever heard one."

Liam wasn't as appreciative of Austin's cynicism today as he would otherwise be.

"You, my friend, have a problem on your hands."

"Tell me something I don't know," Liam mumbled as he stepped out of the car.

They walked into the diner and took a booth near the window.

"I have to tell her the truth." Avery's words rang through his head for the thousandth time.

"You know what's going to happen."

Liam scanned the parking lot. "It has to be done."

"You like her?"

"I like her."

"How much?" Austin picked up a salt shaker and tightened the lid.

Liam wasn't sure he wanted to admit it out loud. If he put it to words then it complicated everything. If he kept it to himself then he could go on with life as if nothing had ever happened.

Then he remembered he would have to see her every weekend at the youth center.

He groaned and banged a fist on the table with restraint.

"Wow." Austin fiddled with a sugar packet. "You're in trouble, man. I've never seen you like this."

He'd never felt like this.

"Why should she know?" Austin shrugged.

"What does that mean?"

"I'm talking about not telling her you're a cop."

"I won't lie to her." Liam felt his stomach clench. Lying was beneath him.

Wasn't it?

"Oh. Right. I forgot you're a holy roller." Austin slouched in his seat.

As if Liam's mood wasn't bad enough, Austin had to go there. "My loyalty is to God first."

"Yeah, well, good luck with that. Guess it's your loss."

Liam gritted his teeth. "If you knew Him, you'd understand."

"Liam, I did know Him. And He turned out to be nothing more than words in a book. Religion is a sham. It's not my thing and if it were up to me it wouldn't be a thing."

"What happened?" Liam asked again. He asked often.

Austin had never fully opened up about that night on the bridge four years ago.

"Ah, you know. You're born, you live, you die." Austin made a gunshot motion with his hand. "Life happens."

Liam could tell there was something holding the kid back from spilling the truth. Probably bitterness. It'll eat away at a heart until God disappeared.

While he'd spent years praying for Austin to see God's mercy for what it really was, he also knew it would take time and effort on Austin's part.

Liam didn't expect him to change. But he hoped to live to see the day his partner called Christ his Savior.

"Look," Austin shrugged. "You don't have to lie to the girl. If you really like her then just give it some time before you tell her. Who knows. Maybe she'll actually find something in you worth loving. Then she won't be able to break it off." He sat up straight. "But what she sees in you, I'll never know."

"You're telling me." Liam crossed his arms and leaned against the table.

Austin's brow wrinkled, his eyes narrowed on the counter where the cash register sat. "Something's wrong," he whispered, his focus roving the nearly-empty diner.

There were a few customers at the tables, but no waitresses among them. The place smelled of coffee but there was none on the tables. A man and woman left without paying.

Liam had seen that look on his partner before and because of it, he'd learned to trust Austin's judgment. There were details Austin noticed before Liam did and things he sensed that others couldn't.

Liam leaned out of the booth and nodded to the last customer in the restaurant. "How long since you've seen a waitress?"

The guy looked past his newspaper and glanced at the clock on the wall. "I don't know. But I'd better get my coffee soon or I'll be taking my business elsewhere."

Liam and Austin left their booth. They went to the counter where waitresses usually stood. Everything seemed normal but oddly quiet. Liam eased up against the kitchen door and listened.

"Where's it at?" A male voice snapped on the other side.

Someone was crying.

"I know you keep it here? Where is it?"

"Okay, okay. Please, don't hurt her. It's here." This came from another male voice.

Liam carefully backed away and turned to Austin. "Holdup. Sounds like one suspect, at least two hostages."

Liam leaned in to his radio and spoke quietly. "I need backup at the Sunshine Diner."

As soon as he relayed the address he twisted the volume down so the dispatcher wouldn't give away his presence.

He gestured to Austin. "Wait for him around back. He might leave out this way but if he doesn't, be ready."

Austin left without another word and Liam moved to the side of the swinging door. If the thief had a gun then Liam didn't want any crossfire with the hostages. He looked back at the diner and found it empty. The older man who hadn't gotten his coffee was shuffling across the parking lot.

"Give me strength," Liam whispered.

He pushed the door inside gently, far enough to see a man's back. A bandana was tied behind his neck, probably covering the lower half of his face. He held one of the waitresses around the middle, a knife to her throat.

The chef struggled to pull a small safe from the freezer into the kitchen. He bent down on one knee and dug a key from his pocket. "This is my life savings. Please don't do this."

"Then you should have buried it in a coffee can," the perp chuckled, jerking the girl until she whimpered against his side.

There were two more waitresses against the wall that Liam could see, but the rest of the kitchen was out of his vision.

The woman held hostage began to wail. She jerked and

started to struggle. Liam silently willed her to stop fighting.

She didn't.

"I'll cut your throat right here if you don't stop."

She wasn't going to stop. She thrashed half-heartedly as if her body were numb.

Heart pumping beneath his bulletproof vest, Liam pushed quietly through the door. He held a finger to his lips, gesturing to the two waitresses who watched him. He stayed against the wall, and moved until he was directly behind the thief.

He could now see that the back door, wide open, was where the guy had come from and where he planned to escape. Austin stood in the shadows, gun drawn, masked by the darkness.

Liam made eye contact with his partner and continued to move along the wall.

Once the money was in his bag, the guy slung the girl away from him and she spun around in tears. When her attention landed on Liam she gasped. The thief turned, eyes wide, and threw the knife. Liam ducked. It clanged against the metal shelf behind him.

"Hands up." Austin stormed in, drawing the guy's focus.

The criminal's hand went inside his jacket and Liam didn't waste a second. He tackled the criminal with all the force of a linebacker he could gather. His shoulder plowed into the thief's midsection and he lifted him up. They both hit the wall with a humph, but Austin was there in the next breath, wrestling him to the ground.

The thief's arm swung twice before Liam realized he held a second knife. The blade came close to Liam's face and near Austin's gun belt. Liam grabbed the arm with both hands and bent it back until the man wailed. The knife dropped and clattered against the floor. The door swung open and uniformed officers flooded the kitchen. They stuck cuffs on the guy and two officers picked him up while Liam caught his breath.

His heart beat wildly in his ears. Sweat trickled down his temple. He heard labored breathing and realized it wasn't coming from him.

It was Austin.

He sat against the wall, a deep wrinkle between his brow. He let out a groan and ripped his uniform open, the buttons falling to the floor.

"No," Liam whispered.

Blood gushed onto Austin's undershirt around his lower abdomen, just below his vest and above his belt. As the pain settled in, he leaned over on his side and moaned.

"We need medics at this location." Liam called over the radio as he moved toward Austin. "We have an officer down."

He dropped the radio and pushed his hand against the wound. "Hang in there, buddy."

Another officer appeared at his side with a first aid kit. He broke it open and Liam pressed a bandage against the wound.

"It's not deep." Austin strained to say, his chest heaving. "It's not deep. It just hurts like heck."

When Liam realized Austin was right, that the wound wasn't fatal, he exhaled. There was an annoying ringing in his ears that he needed to go away.

Ambulance sirens blared over the ruckus of police vehicles and chatter and Liam let his shoulders relax.

"You just don't know how to stay out of trouble do you?"

Austin had the nerve to smile, though his eyes were clenched tight. "You know trouble finds me."

The paramedics came and loaded Austin onto a stretcher. He was carried away before Liam could say another word and the sirens were fading into the distance.

Liam bent down to pick up his radio when he noticed his hands. Austin's blood covered them. The longer he stared at them, the more they shook.

"They say he'll be fine." Police Chief, Raymond

Stafford, approached Liam with a damp towel. "I heard one of the EMTs mention that the blade cut parallel to the abdomen muscles, so there's no permanent damage done. Recovery will be quick."

Liam wiped his hands clean and nodded. He was grateful. "Things could have gone a lot worse."

"This your first time dealing with an injury on the job?"

"With Austin? No. He's been injured before, but not to this magnitude. I have my fair share of scars as well."

"We all do, son," Chief mumbled as he walked away.

Liam looked around at the officers carrying out their duties and taking statements from the chef and waitresses.

In some way, Avery was right.

And it was times like this that reminded him of the same gut-wrenching thought. There were no guarantees that any of them would make it home at the end of the day.

CHAPTER SEVEN

Avery picked up a paint brush and wisped gray strokes against a homemade backdrop. Her mind raced eagerly with a thousand thoughts about the upcoming program the youth had planned.

"See you Monday?" asked one of the volunteers Avery worked with.

"I'll be here." Avery waved as the woman walked off the stage and down the aisle toward the exit. The click of the door latch echoed through the auditorium full of unoccupied seats.

Her thoughts wandered to her apartment where empty cardboard boxes required her attention. A constant reminder as of late. Avery sighed.

She'd talked to Carol yesterday about their Italy plans. Told her she was thrilled about the move. But she hadn't told her that she was reconsidering it.

"I hoped I might find you here."

Avery jumped at the sound of his voice.

Liam stood in front of the stage where the seats ended, hands in his pockets. She noticed he was in jeans instead of gym shorts.

"You found me. What's up?" She turned back to the

canvas.

"Not much…" She could hear him step onto the stage. "Just finished mentoring."

Her brush slowed. Her heart skipped a beat. "Oh yeah?"

"Yeah. I'm about to head home."

"Me too. As soon as I finish this wall." One section left. "How was your day?"

"It was great…you were on my mind a lot."

This man knew how to leave her breathless.

"I was thinking I might ask you out again." He was at her side, watching her hand move back and forth.

"You were thinking?"

He looked into her eyes and she wanted to reach out and touch the stubble along his jaw.

Avery cleared her throat and jerked her attention to the paint can. Her heart sang two different songs. One for this man. Another for a new life in a new city. She wasn't sure which was louder.

"You know. I was thinking about it…" He took the brush from her and continued to paint the white part of the canvas. "But then I figured you've got better things to do on a Saturday night than hang out with the likes of me."

"I could check my schedule but I'm pretty sure I'm free."

"In that case, how do you feel about bowling?"

"Mmm, bowling? I think it's only fair I warn you, my personal best is a seventy-six."

"Then I'll have to show you how to bowl." He gave her a dimpled smile that took her back to that day in February when she had walked out of Bernfeld's thinking she'd never see him again.

And yet here he was. Asking for a second date because apparently she's been on his mind.

He covered the last piece of the canvas. "Is this all?"

She dropped the lid over the paint can and took the

brush from him. "Yeah, I'll wash this out."

"Saturday at seven?"

She pushed the empty cardboard boxes to the back of her mind. She needed more time to think, more time to figure out if Liam was what she wanted for her future. "Sounds great."

She needed more time to figure out if *she* was what he wanted for his.

On her way to the backstage bathroom she stopped short. "Liam?"

He skipped the top stair and stepped back onto the stage. "Yes, ma'am?"

Chivalry was not dead.

"Would you maybe want to go for coffee?" Avery chewed on her lip. This was a first.

"Right now?"

"If you're not busy. I mean, Saturday is a whole two days away. And I know this awesome coffee house not far from here."

"Let's go."

Liam parallel parked in front of L'Espresso Coffee House. He'd passed this place countless times on his patrol. He nearly voiced the thought but stopped short. Now wasn't the right time.

"What do you drink?" She walked in as he held the door.

"Latté." He followed her past a line of waiting customers to the edge of the counter, surprised by her confidence.

"Wait here." She stepped behind the counter.

What just happened? He humbly nodded to the lady

standing at the front of the line. The employees didn't seem to notice as Avery pulled two porcelain cups from a rack on the back wall and set them under the espresso machine. "One shot?"

"Two."

A minute later she handed Liam his coffee and he led her to a table near the window.

"You didn't tell me you work here."

She winked at him over the rim of her cup and he lost himself.

"You do work here, right?"

"Yes." She dabbed a napkin to her lips. "Since I was sixteen."

Impressive. "You told me your life wasn't planned out for you."

She let out a sarcastic chuckle. "The 'plan' was to get married at a young age. My parents and sisters were all married before the age of twenty. And when twenty came and went for me then I put aside my degree in biochemistry and threw myself into this job until it became a career. So the 'plan' changed a little."

"Not much, I hope." He lifted the coffee to his mouth.

She perked an eyebrow. "Not much. Marriage is still a definite possibility for me."

This woman could stir him like no other woman ever had. Liam leaned forward and started to cover her hand with his.

But the bell over the door rang out and Avery looked past him.

"Hi, Avery." A familiar voice stopped Liam's thoughts.

"Miss Dorinda."

Dorinda Jacobs. What was she doing here? *Lord, please don't let her be looking for me.*

Liam stood when Avery did and watched her hug the older woman. Then he dipped his head in a greeting. "Dorinda. How are you?"

"Well, I'll be." She looked at him from his shoes to his

hair. "If Houston ain't small enough."

Liam titled his head toward Avery. "You know each other?"

"I've been coming to L'Espresso 'bout three years now." She placed her hands on her hips, her attention floating between Avery and Liam. "Since I started working the night shift at the hospital. Everybody there knows I need my coffee."

"You know Liam?" Avery's eyes widened.

Liam swallowed. Hard.

"Yes, ma'am. He works with my grandson, JJ, almost every day. Sometimes down at the center. This man is an answer to prayers."

Liam forced a nod, shoving his hands in his pockets.

"JJ." Realization dawned in Avery's eyes. "JJ is your grandson?"

"Have mercy, yes." Dorinda let out a hearty laugh. "My sun rises and sets on that little boy, but I won't deny that he *is* a handful." She arched an eyebrow toward Liam. "Ain't he?"

Liam gave a nervous chuckle. "Sure."

"Pull up a chair, Miss Dorinda." When Avery started to sit, he hesitated. *Oh, Lord please, no.*

"Honey, I wish I could. But I got to get to work." Dorinda leaned a hand against the tabletop. "It looks like you and me have something in common. We both like a man in uniform."

The back of Liam's neck warmed. He slowly melted into his seat. He couldn't catch his breath. This wasn't how it was supposed to happen. Not here. Not now.

"What?" Avery glanced at Liam with a smirk. "No, ma'am. Not me. I have a thing against dating a 'man in uniform'."

There was a question in the wrinkle between Dorinda's arched eyebrows and narrowed eyes as she looked at Liam.

He shook his head as discreetly as he could.

She pursed her lips and she nodded slowly. "I see."

Liam thanked God.

Dorinda turned her attention back to Avery. "Now, miss, might I ask you why?"

Avery lifted her shoulders and let them fall. "I would prefer my man to come home in one piece."

"And a cop—or a man in a uniform—won't come home?"

"Cops, yes, among others." She took a sip of her coffee. "Firemen, soldiers, coast guards. Guys like that. Their jobs require putting their lives on the line. That's not fair to a family. If it were up to me I'd make it so the job requirements include being single."

Liam bowed his head. Was this woman insane? She couldn't go around saying things like that or people would think she'd lost her mind. Everything about her was perfect to him. And then there was this...

He set his hands around his coffee cup and, certain that his secret was safe, he shot a sarcastic smile toward Dorinda.

Dorinda tilted her chin toward Avery. "You're afraid of losing someone close to you?"

After a second, Avery cleared her throat. "Isn't that what we're all afraid of?"

"Now, darling. You listen here. Life is not always fair. Bad things happen to good people and I'll never live long enough to understand why. I've lost two husbands, a daughter, and a grandbaby. But you won't see me give up on love.

"When it comes, it'll come and there's nothing you can do to stop it. And if the Good Lord decides to call that man home then you are going to keep your chin held high, look to the heavens, and thank Him for the time you had with him on earth. And do you know what the ironic part is? It's the hardest thing and it's the easiest thing you'll ever have to do."

Liam wondered, as he stared into Avery's sober face, if he was going to witness her cry. Her eyebrows lifted high, and her lips slightly bent downward. He thought he saw a gentle gloss over her brown eyes, but if it were so, then she did a good job of hiding her emotions. Where he thought he saw a tenderness arising, she was suddenly tough again.

"That's deep, Miss Dorinda. You should consider mentoring at the center. The kids could definitely use someone like you in their lives."

If Liam was any judge of character, what Dorinda said to Avery went in one ear and out the other.

"That sounds right nice, dear, but I'm too busy at the hospital. Night and day it feels like. I'm going to get on, now. Y'all enjoy your date." She winked at Liam and walked away.

"Small world," Avery said.

"It had to be," he mumbled against the cup. He needed to change the subject. "So, uh, you didn't tell me how you got into coffee."

"When my parents finally let me get an after school job, this was the ninth coffee shop I applied to, and they took me in."

"You really like coffee."

"I love it. Not just the way it tastes, but I love the culture, the elegance of it, the way it mixes with other beverages. I've studied it for years."

"It's that serious?"

"Surprisingly, yes. There are classes, schools that teach people to be amazing baristas. I'm planning to go..." Her voice faded fast. Her eyes widened as if she were looking at a ghost.

"Planning to go?" He shouldn't have asked. He could tell it was a mistake in the way she exhaled. Like she'd been holding back a secret that needed to be told.

She looked down at her cup and tapped a white-tipped fingernail against the side. "My sister, Carol, and her husband are moving to Rome. And they want me to go with them. So I can study coffee there."

As if a rod had been shot down his spine, Liam sat up

straighter.

Maybe he'd been wrong. Maybe Avery wasn't the one. This had to be a sign. He wasn't meant for her. And she for him. "What—um, when do you plan to leave?"

"Carol and Branson are leaving right after the baby's born. Next month. But I haven't decided if I want to go with them."

Liam pulled himself to the edge of his chair and tried not to jump to any conclusions. "Rome sounds like a great opportunity. Why the uncertainty?"

"I guess in a way I need to figure out if what I truly want is in Rome."

"Coffee. Family. An adventure of a lifetime. What more could you want?"

She released her hold on the coffee and sat back. Her fingers played with something dangling from her bracelet. "Liam, what is it that *you* want in life?"

That was a question he hadn't thought about in a while. He was content with his career with the police force, although he couldn't tell her that. "I don't know."

He looked down into his coffee. "I love my job. I live in the best city in the world—no offense to Rome. I've got great friends. I would say, besides becoming a better man and a stronger Christian, I would hope to one day get married—"

Liam looked up at Avery, his heart caught somewhere between his lungs and his throat.

"Like I said," she picked up her coffee and grinned as she took a sip. "I need to figure out if what I want is in Rome."

Everything around them disappeared. The crowded coffee shop. The clatter of dishes behind the bar. The traffic outside the window.

The only thing Liam could see was Avery.

Avery and a lifetime.

CHAPTER EIGHT

Avery sat shoulder to shoulder with Liam on the couch in her apartment. She glanced at the clock on the wall and realized bowling was out of the question.

Her sisters and Branson had been there when Liam came to pick her up and now they talked like they had years to catch up on. Avery couldn't say she was entirely disappointed.

Although, she couldn't follow the conversation to save her life. Liam's cologne was like kryptonite to her thoughts. If she were standing, then her knees would no doubt give up on her.

"So you both know Dorinda Jacobs and she didn't introduce y'all?" Carol asked, snapping Avery's thoughts back.

"No." Avery answered as Liam put his arm behind her, along the edge of the couch. It took all she had to keep talking. "Liam has been working with her grandson, JJ, at the youth center for years and Dorinda comes to the coffee shop every week."

"Where'd you two meet again?"

"At the youth center."

"No we didn't." Liam looked over at her.

He sat a little taller than her so she had a perfect view of his clear blue eyes and the dark outline of the brown section. Could he feel the butterflies in her stomach?

"That's right." How could she forget? "We actually met at Bernfeld's. On Valentine's Day."

"I asked her out, but she wouldn't give in."

Grace laughed. "That sounds like Avery. She was never an easy catch."

"You're talking to the queen of hard-to-get." Carol chipped in.

"I wouldn't write that off as a bad thing," Liam said. "If she gave her heart away too easily then I might not get the chance to call her my girl."

Avery's eyes widened with her smile. She'd never been the hopeless romantic type to gush and aww like her sisters. But the man seated at her side was doing a flawless job of winning her heart.

"That is the sweetest." Grace and Carol shared a giggle. "So which one of us are you going to pick for your maid of honor?"

Avery's breath caught in her throat. Her face burned and she was more than sure her cheeks were a dead giveaway. "All right. You're making Liam uncomfortable." She turned to him. "How would you like a personal tour of our six-by-eight balcony just outside that window?"

They stood at the same time and she led the way to the balcony through the sliding glass door. The place was dim and tiny, with just enough room for a few people to admire the view of the warehouse across the street. At least the night chill would help her blush go away.

"You'll have to excuse my sisters. They're a bit imaginative if you haven't noticed." She rested against the metal railing.

"I noticed." He leaned beside her and mirrored her stance. "So which one are you going to pick?"

"Which what?"

"Which sister is going to be your maid of honor?"

And the blushing came back. "I can't believe you brought that with you."

He laughed and she savored the sound. "It's a common question."

Though it was cut short, his hair was kind of messy, like he'd run his fingers through it.

She liked this guy. A lot. Probably a little more than a lot. And the more she got to know him the more attractive he became to her. "You going to call me your girl?"

He bit back a smile and dropped his head. "I knew I'd have to take a leap of faith on that one."

"That was a pretty big leap for a second date."

"Third if you count coffee."

"And then if you add up the hours we've spent at the youth center together."

"And Valentine's Day." He bumped her shoulder with his and leaned forward over the railing, elbows braced.

"Then we've known each other for, like, years."

"At least a few."

She held back a laugh and let the silence fall over them. Or rather, the rush of traffic and occasional honking horn that passed as silence in the heart of Midtown Houston.

She scanned the yard across the street, the one she'd seen a thousand times. Her eyes roved the street lights parallel to her third-story home. Then she found Liam staring at her. "What?"

He hesitated. "What are you afraid of?"

She lifted her shoulders. "Nothing."

"You have to be afraid of something." His eyes searched her through the darkness. "You can't be fearless."

"What are *you* afraid of?"

"I don't know." He looked up at the sky. "I guess disappointment, rejection, humiliation. Having my mistakes thrown back in my face. What most people fear."

"I don't fear disappointment."

Liam scoffed. "Okay. What do you fear, then?"

"Spiders."

"No. Absolutely not. Everybody hates spiders. It has to be personal to you—something that paralyzes you."

Avery combed her fingers through her hair. This was getting intimate. Made her skin crawl. But if she liked this guy, if she had a chance for a future with Liam then she'd have to cross this bridge sooner or later.

"The absence of something—or someone—you love. Never being able to touch them, hear them, see them. Knowing you'll never be near them." She pulled in a long, sturdy breath. "I once had an imaginary friend that I loved. It was the worst experience of my life."

His brow furrowed, a tell-tale sign that he knew what she was thinking. "Is that why you won't date guys with dangerous jobs? You're afraid of losing them?"

"There's a little bit more to it than that, but yes. That's basically the reason."

"Tell me."

She didn't want to. She wanted to play it off. Joke about it. Change the subject or go back inside.

But he deserved to know.

"I told you that Grace was married before?"

He nodded.

She sighed. "Nathan was like a brother to us all. Me. Carol. Grace. We grew up together, so he was like part of our family. It made perfect sense that he and Grace were meant to be together. So when they got married it was like one of the best things that could have happened to our family, right?"

The compassion she found in Liam's eyes gave her the strength to go on.

"When Nathan died, he took a part of us with him. All of us. Me and Carol, we lost a brother that day. My parents lost a son. Grace was pregnant with their first kid, but, uh…" Her throat closed up. Her eyes stung. But she forbade the tears. "She lost the baby."

She looked down at her hands. "Grace…I'll never

forget the way she screamed when they told her he was gone. It'll be eight years in August and I still have nightmares about that day."

She heard him exhale a long breath.

"It took us months before we could actually talk like a family again. Laugh together. But Grace didn't start healing until—actually, until a few years ago. She's had a hard road. One that I don't want to take."

"How did Nathan die?"

"The roof caved in when his company went inside. They—" She chewed the inside of her cheek. "They checked the structure of the building before they went in. It was supposed to be safe, but it fell anyway. He was pinned under a support beam. They couldn't even find him until the house had been extinguished."

Liam straightened to his full height and whispered, "He was a fireman."

"There's not a day that goes by that I don't think about him."

"Avery," he whispered.

"That's why I keep my distance from guys like that. I watched Grace fall so hard it broke her. She hasn't been the same since. I can't. I won't."

"Avery, baby, you can't let that hold you back from life. From love."

"I'm not." She assured him. "There's not love in me for a guy like that. I have no desire—"

"It's not about desire or finding it in you. It's about faith. It's about trusting that God has a plan."

"I know He does. I've seen it in Grace. I see Him working in her every day. But that's a bridge that I can't cross, Liam. It happened to her. Chances are, it won't happen to me. Even if it could, I won't let it."

His head dropped, his eyes closed. Could he see things her way? Or did he find her unreasonable?

"Avery." His voice dripped with empathy when he looked at her. "One day you're going to find that guy standing in front of you. The guy you've been avoiding for eight years. You'll have to make a choice. Fall in love? Dream about a future with him? The possibility of a life together? Saying 'I do' at the end of the aisle? The kids you'll share, jumping into your arms? Growing old with him with the understanding that you're going to face hard times and your hair is going to turn gray and his will probably fall out, but you know there is nobody else on the face of the earth that fits more perfectly in your life than he does. And when it's all said and done you realize you wouldn't have it any other way."

"And my other option would be spending a lifetime trying to forget the color of his coffin."

"I don't agree with you."

"I didn't expect you to." She cocked her head and looked into his eyes. "But this is something that's important to me…Does this change things?"

A slow, confident smile stretched across his face. "The way I feel about you? Not a chance."

In that moment, she thought she saw him lean forward, as if he were going to close the gap between them. She waited, begging her heart to be still.

He hesitated. Then he straightened.

Disappointing. But it was understandable. Maybe it was because he knew her sisters were watching.

Or maybe he wanted to take things slow. She didn't mind. In fact, if that were the reason, then it made her more inclined to wait for that kiss.

"I think I'm in love with you," he whispered.

Her chest tingled with delight. The butterflies in her stomach turned into a hurricane. "Let me know when you're done thinking."

His smile broadened. He chewed on his bottom lip. "All right. I love you."

"Based on what, exactly?" She couldn't help but laugh. "I just gave you my life story. The sappy, pathetic version. And you found something in that worth loving?"

"Yeah." He nodded slowly, his eyes roving her face. "You don't make it hard."

"Hmm. I guess I'm going to have to step up my game."

She felt his hand around her wrist, where his warm touch slid down her palm and his fingers tangled through hers. "If you do, rest assured I won't give up."

She grinned and felt a shiver go up her back. "Grace would be my maid of honor. Carol would be my matron of honor because she's married."

"Yeah?" He whispered, street lights reflecting in his eyes. "Which means?

She tightened her grip. "I love you, too."

CHAPTER NINE

Liam turned his truck onto Dorinda's road with JJ on the passenger side, feasting on a kids' meal. He parked on the street in front of the house and, like always, followed JJ inside.

Dressed in scrubs, Dorinda stood in the kitchen, looking into an oval mirror hanging above a small table pushed against the wall.

"How was your day, Dorinda?"

"Honey, my day's just getting started." She pulled her scalp-hugging curls back into a thick ponytail. "My neighbor'll be here in about five minutes to watch JJ."

JJ sat on the sofa, a box of fries and half a burger in his lap.

"Yes, ma'am. I'll get out of your way. Y'all have a good night."

"Not so fast, Liam Reed."

Liam stopped short and arched an eyebrow. That tone hadn't sent chills down his spine since his grandma was alive.

Dorinda tapped a finger against the table and eased into a chair. "Come have a seat for a second."

Liam obliged. "Am I in trouble?"

"I don't know. We'll see."

The chair scraped across the floor as he pulled it out.

Dorinda's petite shoulders hunched slightly. "Explain to me what Avery thinks you do for a living."

His heart dropped into his tennis shoes. Smile gone, he gulped. "I know I'm in the wrong."

"We both know that. You got all your senses, Liam, I haven't doubted that. I just want to know what you've done with them."

He propped his elbows on the tabletop and swept his hands down his face. "I fell in love. I fell hard."

"I figured as much," she bobbed her head.

"It's just, every time I decide to tell her the truth, it doesn't feel right. When I wake up in the morning, I tell myself I'm going to do it today, but...when I see her." He shook his head and looked into Dorinda's dark brown eyes. "I don't want to lose her."

"Are you sure you will?"

"Oh yeah. Avery. She's a stubborn woman. Her beliefs are her identity. And she believes that a job like mine will take me away from her. I can see where she's coming from, but I don't agree with it."

"Neither do I. But you realize this comes from an underlying problem, don't you?"

He nodded. "Her brother-in-law was a firefighter. She lost him to a fire."

Dorinda laid her arms along the table's edge and locked her fingers together. "That would explain it."

"I don't know what to do."

"Yes, you do."

"I don't want to do it." He didn't even want to think about it.

"Do you have a choice?"

No, he didn't. Avery deserved the truth. But the thought of never seeing her again was like a punch to the throat. He scrubbed his hands down his face again and felt like he was drowning.

"Baby, don't you know it's Avery's job to trust God with your life?"

"Yes, ma'am."

"So don't you think it's your job to trust Him with Avery?"

He hadn't thought of it like that. "I guess Avery and I have a lot more in common than I thought."

"You both need to learn how to trust each other. And once you tell her the truth, she'll need to learn that trust all over again."

Liam rubbed a hand across his temple. "That's only if she'll talk to me again."

"You look here, Liam Reed. Don't you worry about what *could* happen, or what *might* happen. You focus on what you feel in here." She pressed her fingers against her heart. "I see the struggle in your eyes, honey. Your convictions are holding you down like a snake. But you've been compromising your faith for your flesh. Stop that."

The door opened wide and a young woman Liam recognized as a neighbor walked in. "Hi, Miss Dorinda."

"Just a minute, Bethany, I'm lecturing." Dorinda never took her eyes off Liam. "Sweetheart, don't you want a love that's built on truth and honesty? Don't you want a marriage based on God's plan for your life? Would you trade that for the lie you're living now?"

He closed his eyes and cringed. "No, ma'am."

"You may very well have to come to grips with the fact that Avery might not be the one for you after all."

He fought the urge to grit his teeth.

"You need to stop fighting with this. Tell her the truth. And make His will your first priority. Because when you surrender, everything will start to fall into place. And last of all, walk me to my car."

He couldn't help but smile. Liam left his seat, said bye to JJ and the neighbor, and walked Dorinda out the door and across the yard.

"You don't have to take my advice if you don't want.

But you done so much for me and JJ, I just thought I'd repay the favor."

Liam was grateful. "I'm not sure where I'd be without you, Dorinda."

"I feel the same about you."

Liam sighed as he stopped beside his truck. "I need to trust Avery."

Dorinda glared at him, eyebrows raised. "You need to trust God."

CHAPTER TEN

Liam leaned forward in the driver's seat and glanced at the ribbons of sun spilling through the clouds. It was a perfect day for what he needed to do.

"Are you sure the timing is right?" Avery rubbed her fingers against that long charm hanging from her bracelet. A sign that she was nervous.

"Of course it's right." He rubbed a hand over his jaw. "Stop worrying."

"I'm not worrying. I just want to make a good first impression."

"Don't worry about making a good impression. You've impressed me and that's all that matters."

He didn't tell her she wasn't actually going to meet his dad.

She couldn't.

"Why that one?" He gestured to her hands.

She followed his question to her wrist and dropped the charm as if she hadn't realized she'd been touching it. "It's smoother than the other ones."

"What's it mean?"

She lifted her arm at an awkward angle so she could see it better. "It says trust."

Trust. That's exactly what Liam needed her to do right now. His chest tensed as he turned under the iron arch sign that read *Living River Cemetery*.

He heard her intake of breath. Her shoulders fell and she dropped her charm. "Is this where your dad is?"

Liam released his white-knuckle grip on the steering wheel and put the truck in park. "Yeah."

"I'm sorry." It was a solemn, unimposing apology.

He met her in front of the truck and she slipped her hand into his, no doubt noticing his damp palms. "Take me to see him?"

He wanted to plant a kiss on her sweet smile but thought better of it. It wouldn't be fair. At least, not until she knew the truth about him.

He admired the way she hung back and let him lead her down the walkway, between the rows of tombstones and flowers.

"It's only Dad here." He gave her a glance to gauge her reaction. "My mom left us when I was little. I barely remember her."

A tiny line appeared between Avery's brows. Her smile disappeared.

Liam stopped in front of a freshly mowed patch of earth marked by a four-foot-tall headstone, and tugged Avery to his side.

"He wanted to be laid near his dad." Liam gestured to a pair of nearby graves that belonged to his grandparents.

He rubbed his thumb across Avery's knuckles and watched her eyes travel over his father's name. William George Reed.

Her fingers slipped away from his and she approached the tombstone, careful not to stand over the place where his father was buried. She crouched down and touched the picture imprinted on the bottom corner of the stone.

"He looked like you."

Liam remembered him well. Aside from the white

hair and hazel eyes, they were very close in appearance. "Dad had a few pounds on me."

She smiled and her hand dropped. "It's very nice to meet you, Mr. Reed. I'll admit you have raised an amazing son. But I'm sure you already know that. I'm blessed to have met him. You probably had something to do with that, didn't you?"

Liam chuckled, the sting of tears in his eyes.

"Thank you, sir, for—" She went still, like she forgot to breathe.

Did she see what he saw?

His eyes roved over the badge beside his father's date of death.

"Liam?" She slowly stood. "Your dad was a cop?"

"Yeah." He waited for the question he knew she would ask.

"How did he die?"

"In the line of duty." He could still see the mile-long line of traffic stretching down the Houston highways for his funeral. "He was responding to a shootout and got caught in the crossfire."

Liam had been patrolling the Third Ward, too far away from the shootout to be with his father when he took his last breath. Like a knife through his chest, Liam felt the pain of losing his dad all over again. Something he'd become numb to over the years.

"I'm so sorry." Her voice dripped with sorrow and empathy.

In a second she was in his arms, holding on tight. Whether it was compassion for him or strength for her, he didn't know. He pulled her close, nonetheless.

When she drew away, she took both his hands in hers. "Can I...can I pray for you?"

His pulse raced. He'd never had a woman pray for him besides Dorinda. And he'd yet to hear Avery pray. "Right now?"

"Yeah," she said, tilting her head sideways.

"Of course."

Avery tightened her grip on him and bowed her head. "Father," her voice turned soft and sweet. "I thank You for the time Liam's dad had on this earth. I understand how hard it can be to lose someone we love. Thank You for bringing Liam to a place of strength and understanding. I praise You for the things you're doing in his life and where You're taking him. I ask that You would continue to bring comfort and peace to him. We thank You and we love You. In Jesus' name."

"Amen," he whispered.

This woman had his heart and he didn't mind.

"It had to be hard for you."

Liam knew she could relate.

Which is why he chose this route to tell her.

"My dad was an inspiration to me. To a lot of people."

"I can imagine he was. Nathan was like that. There wasn't a soul alive that didn't love him."

"Yeah. That's how Dad was. I wanted to do everything he did. I wanted to be just like him…"

Liam watched her closely. She was listening to him, but she wasn't reading between the lines.

Did she understand at all? Why should she? He was dancing around the truth.

"Avery. I'm not much different from my dad."

She had a faraway gaze. "You both have hearts of gold."

"And we both have a—" *badge.*

He nearly said it. But the cry of her cell phone stopped him.

"You should get that."

She was hesitant, maybe even regretful. She pulled her phone from her pocket and checked the screen.

Liam licked his lips. Why was it so hot out here?

"It's Grace," she mumbled as she lifted the phone to her ear. "Hey."

The look on her face changed from nonchalance to shock. She looked up at Liam with a grin. "Carol's water broke."

CHAPTER ELEVEN

Three days later, Avery, with Liam at her side, stepped into Carol and Branson's home to visit little Jeremy Branson Ellert Jr. again after being discharged from the hospital.

"I'm so glad you could make it." Carol sat on the recliner with Jeremy against her, tucked beneath a nursing cover.

Avery felt Liam's hand tighten in hers and he almost stopped short.

She bit back a smile and led him to the couch furthest from Carol and the baby. "How's the little guy doing?"

"Hungry," Branson said as he sat on the arm of Carol's chair. "I've never seen a baby that could eat so much."

"Mmm." Avery bit back a laugh when Liam started shaking his leg. "He's a true Sanders."

"That's what I told Branson. He doesn't think three girls could eat as much as we did."

"She's serious. We have a love for food. Grace loves veggies, for Carol it's anything with meat, and I'm a sugar addict."

"Which would be why I found you in the candy aisle

when we met," Liam said, wrapping his arm around her.

"You have my sweet tooth to thank."

Carol finished nursing and started to shift around as she situated Jeremy. Liam suddenly found something interesting on the other side of the room.

Avery wanted to tell him that nursing was a natural gift from God. Being an only child and thirty-two-year bachelor, she could understand his discomfort.

Carol settled baby Jeremy against her shoulder and patted his tiny back. "So how are things out in the world? I feel like I haven't been out in ages."

"You haven't missed much," Avery said, anxious to get Jeremy in her arms.

When the baby burped, Carol started to rock him. "Liam, you didn't get a chance to hold Jeremy at the hospital, did you? Would you like to?"

Liam had a caught-off-guard smile. "Sure."

He went to Carol and carefully took the baby from her.

"I'm going to go wash up." Carol wiped a rag against the blotch on her T-shirt as she and Branson walked into the kitchen.

Instead of sitting, Liam went to the window where the sunlight spilled over the newborn.

Avery went weak at the knees.

The baby was sweet.

But Liam was stunning.

He swayed slowly from side to side, his eyes trained on Jeremy. She'd never seen him smile like that before. It was a small smile but enthusiastic. As if he was the happiest man on earth.

He would make an amazing daddy.

Liam was everything a woman could want. Sure, he was blunt to a fault, he could be so lax and quiet at times that it made her want to scream. They argued about silly little things like the word irregardless as opposed to regardless and which route was the quickest to the heart of

Houston.

But he was a dream of a man.

All six-foot-two of him. Strong and masculine. Yet he had the grace and gentleness to rock a newborn to sleep. His lips moved slightly as he whispered something to the baby Avery couldn't hear. He was strong. Confident. Virile. And completely in control.

Avery was hopelessly in love.

She left the couch and went to stand with him. She ran her fingers along Jeremy's soft scalp and his feathery strands of hair.

"He's beautiful, isn't he?" Liam whispered.

"So are you." Avery swallowed, aware that she'd actually said it. "Um, I take it you hope to have kids one day?"

His smile turned into a grin as he searched her face, still swaying back and forth. "So long as you're their mother."

Eyes wide, mouth slack, Avery's heart skipped a beat. Her knees buckled beneath her.

"Wow. I've actually witnessed you speechless. I'd call that a milestone."

"I think you're the only man who's ever made me speechless." She rubbed her damp palms against her jeans. Her cheeks were warm. Probably red.

Liam leaned forward and pressed a kiss to the baby's forehead.

She wondered if she could ever love anyone more.

"The baby's here," his smile faded. "What does that mean for you?"

She looked around at the storage boxes that sat ready to be shipped overseas. "The flight leaves in a week and a half. But I haven't packed yet. If someone were to ask me to stay, I might be inclined."

Liam came closer. With the baby cradled between them, he hooked a finger beneath her chin and lifted her face. "Avery Sanders, you've captivated me."

Her heart pounded so hard she feared she might miss the word she longed to hear.

His solemn gaze locked on her. "Stay."

CHAPTER TWELVE

Even though the parking lot was packed, Avery was walking on air. Not a single vacant space could be found near the front of the youth center Friday afternoon, but that didn't daunt her joy.

Liam had asked her to stay.

She trekked from the back side of the lot and glanced up at the banner hanging under the sign.

Consumed Youth Community Center Theatre Department Presents Flowers for Autumn *2:00 Friday & Saturday.*

Avery had gotten off work early to be here. Even still she was running late.

She rolled up the sleeve of her blouse and waited for a car to pass. When she looked up she found a police cruiser sitting in front of the center doors. Her eyebrows peaked with her curiosity. Hopefully nobody was hurt. Or in trouble.

An officer wearing aviator shades stood beside the doors, thumbs tucked behind his belt. He looked too young to be a cop but his uniform proved otherwise.

"Ma'am."

"Is everything all right?" She noticed his nametag read *Brooks*.

"Yes, ma'am. My partner is dropping off a kid. Nothing to worry about."

She smiled and he dipped his head as he pulled the door open for her.

Kellie stepped out of her office shuffling a stack of mail. "Wait a second. I have a handout for you." She stepped back into her office and returned with a paper. "Ready for the program?"

"Yep. Will you be there?"

"Of course...Liam's here."

Avery paused. "Yeah?"

"Just came in."

Avery stepped into the hallway. The paper was an announcement for the Fourth of July cookout coming up in a few months. Kind of early, she thought. But she looked forward to sharing it with Liam now that she was here to stay.

The thought brought a smile to her face.

The doors at the end of the hall clicked as someone came through them.

When Avery looked up, she stopped dead in her tracks. The announcement slid from her fingers and flittered to the floor. "Liam?"

Liam slowly came to a stop, eyes wide, mouth slack. Somehow he looked taller. Broader. Stronger.

He wore a police uniform.

"I can explain," he said.

She prayed he was joking. Mocking her. Anything.

But she'd seen the other officer outside with the car.

"I can't believe you..." She couldn't breathe. The air whooshed out of her. This wasn't happening.

"Avery, let me explain."

Her stomach turned upside down. She wanted to run, but her legs were weak. Her chest ached deep down around her heart. Memories from every minute she'd spent with Liam forced themselves to the front of her thoughts and choked her. Every second she thought she knew who he was. "You lied to me."

He closed the distance between them. Each step fell in line with the drum of her heartbeats. "I never told you I wasn't a cop. I just didn't tell you that I was."

"It's still a lie." Her eyes stung. Her heart stung. His deception burned her to the core.

"I should have told you."

A sarcastic laugh croaked from her suddenly dry lips. "But you couldn't find the time?"

"I wanted to tell you—I tried to tell you. Many times. But it seemed like every time I tried, something would come up."

"Something more important than telling me who you really are?" She turned to leave, her hands shaking.

He caught up with her quick and grabbed her arm.

"You knew." She pulled away from him. "I told you I don't date cops. You knew that. You knew why I couldn't date someone like—"

"I wanted to tell you the truth."

"Honestly, Liam—"

His radio came on and a voice rattled something off. She watched him as he listened intently, his shoulders straight, his eyebrows low. His focus scanned over her face but didn't really look *at* her.

"Officer down," the dispatcher said.

Avery's blood ran cold. Her heart tore at her chest.

Liam was stunningly calm. "I've got to go. Can I call you later?"

"Don't bother."

He didn't let another second pass before he was gone. The air around her seemed charged, but dull at the same time. Like the calm before the storm.

CHAPTER THIRTEEN

A drop of rain drizzled down the window in Avery's apartment. Nothing made sense.

Her thoughts ached for answers, but her heart warned her the questions were better left unasked.

The TV in the background dulled her mind. Thank God.

God. He seemed to be the only one who hadn't abandoned her in this mess. She'd spent days chasing her anger in circles. But somewhere deep down she knew He was looking out for her.

Someone knocked on the door and Grace left the couch to answer it. The sound of someone clearing their throat pulled Avery's attention away from the window to Liam standing in the doorway.

Decked out in his police uniform, he still looked just as manly as ever.

And just as terrifying.

Grace's gestured and he stepped inside.

"You're not welcome here." Avery wanted to push him out but she didn't trust herself to move toward him. "I don't have anything to say to you."

He rubbed the back of his neck. "Can we talk, Avery?"

"I told you, I have nothing to say." Her voice cracked, so she lowered it. "It's over, Liam. There's nothing between us."

He sighed. "I never lied to you."

"And you didn't tell me the truth, either." She despised him for stealing her heart. She despised herself for giving it away so easily.

Behind Liam, Avery saw Grace leave the room.

"I'm sorry. I was wrong for not telling you." His tone became more confident. "If I had it to do over again I'd do it right. Even if it meant losing you. But losing you this way, Avery, is killing me."

"That's the choice you made."

He sighed again, this time with less patience. "Avery, be honest with me. If I didn't own this uniform would we be standing here right now?"

Her throat closed, and her eyes burned until he turned to a blur. She should have seen this coming. He was too good to be true. Why did she have to fall for him so easily?

Her teeth ground together. She made a promise that this would never happen again. Her chest ached at the thought.

The words "officer down" echoed in her head. Images of flying bullets, the scent of gunpowder made her stomach turn. Losing him… "I won't let you do this to me."

He made the mistake of coming closer. "Tell me. I need to know."

In that moment, everything inside her burned. She hated him and loved him in the same breath.

She reached out and shoved him, but it didn't do much good, he held steady. "You never took one second to think about how this would hurt me?"

She didn't want to bear her heart to him like this, but the words tumbled out anyway. "You never thought enough about me to stop lying and say 'Look, Avery, I'm not who I said I was.' You didn't think about what this would cost me." She pressed her fingertips to her heart. "You only wanted to save yourself the pain of breaking up with me. How did that work out for you?"

His jaw ticked. "It wouldn't have changed your mind about me."

"You're right. But this way is a lot easier, isn't it?" She hid her aggravation behind a smile. "Let's face it. We were never going to make it even if you weren't a cop."

He had the gall to chuckle. "Don't say that, Avery. You and I both know if it wasn't for your ridiculous idea to not date guys like me we'd be on our way down the aisle."

"You're kidding yourself."

"Am I? You're the one living a fairytale where nobody dies. Just because you don't marry a man with a job like mine doesn't guarantee that he'll come home at the end of the day."

Liam had shattered her heart. He could see it in her eyes. A million tiny pieces. Though she didn't cry. He'd yet to see her cry, that beautiful, stubborn woman.

He knew where she'd developed her complex, her fear of dating guys like him, but he wasn't going to apologize for what he said. It was true, whether she wanted to hear it or not. And while it was his lie that brought them to this point, it would be her choice to break them apart or quit hiding behind a fantasy.

She needed to get over it.

Then it hit him.

Avery wasn't over Nathan's death. She was still mourning. He didn't know why, but she was.

It made sense now.

"I'll make it clear for both of us," she whispered.

"We're done. There's nothing between us and there will never be anything between us."

She walked away, down the hall, where he heard a door barely click shut. He would rather she slam it.

How had things gotten turned around? He'd come to apologize, but now he'd only made things worse. For both of them.

He turned to leave.

"I'm sorry that it had to be like this." Grace said, leaning against the wall in the hallway. "I have to admit, I don't know where she would have gotten such a standard for dating guys. I mean, personally I think she's scared to marry anyone at all, not just—" She gestured to his uniform. "But to pass up on a chance at love over this…"

She really didn't know? "It's because of your husband."

"Nathan?" She stepped out of the hallway, into the light where he could see her better. "Why?"

"When Nathan died Avery said she lost a brother that day. And uh…" He lowered his gaze. "You lost a baby. I'm sorry, ma'am."

"That's why she broke up with you?"

"She's convinced that since your husband passed away that every man with a dangerous job is going to die."

It was coming to him now. Clearly. "I think you're right. She knows better than that. It's not about marrying a guy like me. She has a fear of losing anyone close to her."

She nodded and he could see understanding light her eyes.

"I just wish there was a way to fix this mess."

"Avery is probably going to kill me for saying this." She grimaced and for a second, despite her light brown hair pulled back into a ponytail, she looked a bit like Avery. "Don't give up on her. If you really love her like you say you do, and you seriously want to fix things between you, don't stop showing her that you love her."

His chest stirred with hope.

"She's a tough nut to crack, but she's a sweetheart underneath. You just got to figure her out. She'll come around."

He shook his head. "You really believe that?"

"I do. She's going to need some time, lots of it. And you'll need to give her a reason to trust you again. Starting off a relationship with a lie isn't exactly paradise."

He'd already journeyed to that conclusion.

"But she does love you. Avery's almost thirty and you're the first guy in her life that she's talked about marrying."

The air whooshed out of him. "She did?"

"Oh, yeah. Often. And I can't tell you how many times I've caught her smiling to herself. In fact," she paused, her lips pursed as if she shouldn't go on. "I realized it the other day. In between the time you two met on Valentine's Day and when you met at the center, there were a lot of days when she would smile, too."

If Grace was right, then there was still hope. He needed to think. "Thank you, ma'am."

He started to leave, but stopped in the doorway. "Grace, I thank you for your husband's service, to our city and also to our country."

Her brow wrinkled. She gave him a small smile. "And thank you for your service, as well. I'm proud of what you do."

He gave her a single nod and left.

CHAPTER FOURTEEN

Liam rubbed his palms against his jeans. He sat by himself at L'Espresso Coffee House, his heart banging against his chest. Waiting, he scanned the glass storefront.

Avery came into view.

The sight of her made him inhale, pulling himself up straight. She was beautiful.

She wore a vest over a tank top and tucked a strand of hair behind her ear. He could hardly contain his admiration for her when she held the door for a customer.

Liam went unnoticed as she walked in. She stepped behind the counter and disappeared through a doorway.

The coffee shop wasn't terribly crowded, but that didn't stop the nerves from turning his stomach.

Avery emerged from the back wearing an apron. Two more employees were working but at the moment were out of sight. She stood with her back to Liam, filling a machine with coffee.

"Lord, please let Grace be right," he whispered and stood.

Halfway to the counter, he stopped. Right in the middle of the shop. He exhaled deeply and disregarded the onlookers burning holes in him with their curious stares.

"I'm not giving up on you."

Avery paused, as still as a rock. She slowly looked over her shoulder and studied him, as if to confirm his presence.

"I've already apologized, so I'm not here to do that," he told her, ignoring the heat that crawled down his neck. "I'm here to tell you that I can't live without you, Avery."

He pulled his badge out of his pocket and tossed it to her over the counter. "This belongs to you."

She caught it and rubbed her thumb across the imprint.

He wasn't bluffing. If she would have him then he would give up the force. He'd settle down and take a job that wasn't as self-sacrificing.

Her eyes met his and she hesitated. Long enough to kindle his hope.

She tossed it back over the counter and he caught it against his chest. "Keep it."

Liam's heart leapt into his throat. So, that was her answer? "I just gave you everything you've asked for, Avery."

Her eyes flittered across the countertop, across the floor in front of him. Was she finally coming around? Or would she tear him down?

"Liam, if I said I still love you after all of this..." She sounded certain. Confident. Cold. "...I'd be lying."

Point blank. He felt like he'd been shot. There was no mercy in her voice. He wanted to lie to himself and say there was no love for her in his heart. But he knew better—and she knew it, too.

Grace was wrong. Avery couldn't be won over. She was too stubborn, too distant for her own good. He wanted to save her, a damsel drowning in sorrow. But she wouldn't let herself be saved.

Humiliation seeped over him and burned him from the outside in. The realization of everything he'd risked appeared before him. Along with everything he was losing.

She didn't say another word. There was no attempt to justify what she felt. No apology. No goodbyes.

It nearly killed him.

Liam let his pride go. He turned around and walked out of the coffee shop. Somehow he would have to let Avery Sanders become part of his past.

CHAPTER FIFTEEN

The next day, his shift nearly over, Liam got a call over his radio about a suspicious person in a familiar area.

"Ten four." He glanced at Austin. "Description sounds like Charlie Jacobs."

"What I was thinking. Wouldn't hurt to scope it out."

There were two men at the scene. Both walking down the sidewalk away from the cruiser. Liam flipped the siren on and off to get their attention.

It took them too long to come to a stop. When they didn't turn around Liam tightened his fist around the steering wheel and he put it in park. He and Austin stepped out of the car but stayed behind their open doors.

"How y'all doing?"

They finally turned around. One of the men was unknown. The other—whom Liam recognized as Charlie—reached into his pocket.

Liam loosened his gun. "Keep your hands where I can see 'em, Charlie."

Charlie didn't listen.

The other guy shifted from side to side.

"Got him, Austin?"

"I got him." Austin watched intently.

Liam pulled his gun up. "Charlie, get your hands out

of your pockets, now. I'm telling you once."

Charlie removed his hands slowly from his pockets and lifted them, fisted, in the air. The unknown male took off like a lightning bolt. Austin pursued.

Liam kept his focus on Charlie, his chest heaving. "Put your hands behind your head and face away from me."

Charlie reluctantly obliged. He interlocked his fingers and turned around.

"Now walk backward."

Charlie shifted from one foot to the other but he wasn't moving.

"Let's go, Charlie. Follow my directions and everything will go smoothly."

"I ain't going back, Reed."

Liam leaned in to his radio. "Requesting backup." He lifted his voice again. "We can talk about that in a minute. Now walk backward toward the sound of my voice."

Charlie pushed off and ran.

Liam slammed his door and shoved his gun in the holster as he followed suit. Charlie's legs pumped as he passed cars parallel parked in the street and yards where kids were playing.

"Stop, Charlie!"

The guy picked up speed and headed east.

Liam knew where he was going. He couldn't let him get there.

Charlie's arm went over his head and he chucked something onto a nearby lawn. Liam's heart raced as he closed in on Charlie, but he was too far out of reach.

Dorinda's house came into view beyond a patch of trees. Liam steered off the path and broke through the trees, ignoring the branches reaching for him. He cut across Dorinda's yard when Charlie did. They stepped onto the porch at the same time and Liam wrapped him up.

They fell through the old, splintered door and it

ripped off its hinges. Liam landed against his shoulder, Charlie beneath him. They both grunted with the impact. Dorinda screamed bloody murder and JJ wailed.

Liam got to his knees and wrestle Charlie's hands behind his back.

The guy didn't put up much of a fight. Liam clipped the cuffs on Charlie and grabbed his radio.

"One suspect in custody," he managed between rapid breaths.

Backed against the living room wall, Dorinda held JJ in her arms. Moisture glistened on her cheeks.

"You all right?" he asked.

She nodded adamantly.

When backup arrived minutes later, Liam had another officer frisk Charlie and get him into a cruiser. After he found the discarded drug paraphernalia and met Austin back at the car with the other suspect, he returned to Dorinda's house for a report.

She was compliant but distant, more so than she'd ever been before. About to leave and well past the end of his shift, Liam stopped to inspect the curtain now hanging over the empty doorframe.

"You gonna catch heat for that?" Dorinda gestured toward the door, her arms hugging her midsection.

"I shouldn't." Warm air was already flooding the place. "I'll come by in a few hours to replace it."

"Don't worry about it." Her voice cracked. Unlike her.

"This isn't going to last through the night, especially if it rains." Liam gestured to the sheet and tucked the notebook in his waistband. He looked around. "Where's JJ?"

"His room." She tilted her chin toward the hallway. "He'll be fine. He's seen his daddy get arrested before."

If Liam had any control over the situation he would have kept Dorinda and JJ far away from it. But this was the route Charlie took.

She refused to make eye contact with Liam and hadn't since he'd set foot in the house. Maybe it was too much for her heart.

"You going to be all right?"

Her jaw ticked. She looked over the shards of wood lying in a swept pile, her forehead wrinkled. Her gaze suddenly turned hard. "I can't do it again."

Liam dropped his attention to the scuffed floor. "You probably won't have to. With this charge he'll be facing prison time."

"I don't mean Charlie."

Liam shook his head. "I don't understand."

Her eyes frantically searched the walls as if seeking answers. "I can't do it. I can't raise another boy. JJ is on the same path his father took."

"JJ is a long way from being like his dad. Don't hold Charlie's sins against your grandson."

"Liam." She finally looked at him, daggers reflecting in her eyes. "Charlie was arrested for the first time when he was twelve years old. JJ has already seen the back of your police car more than once. And he's only ten. I got no idea what I did to make him turn out like this. And the one thought that keeps me up at night is 'what did I do?'"

She shook her head firmly. "I don't trust myself, Liam. I don't trust myself to raise JJ. I don't know what I did wrong the first time. How am I supposed to do it any different this time?"

CHAPTER SIXTEEN

By the time Avery made it to her apartment, the wind had wreaked havoc on her hair. She smoothed the tangled mess as she checked to see if the door was unlocked.

Grace was home, sitting on the couch with a mug and a magazine. "Hey. How was your day?"

"Same as every day. How was yours?" Avery dropped her bag on the counter and snagged a water bottle from the fridge.

"Can we talk?"

That was never a good question. "Are you kicking me out?"

"Rent is fourteen hundred dollars. I can't afford to kick you out."

Avery gently lowered her water bottle and twisted the lid back on. "You do remember that I'm moving to Rome tomorrow?"

"I know. I was being sarcastic. You think you'd recognize it."

Avery plopped down on the loveseat.

"You're still leaving?"

"Of course. I thought we talked about this."

"Yeah." Grace set her mug on the coffee table. "I

thought you changed your mind after you met Liam."

"Is this what we're talking about, because I have better things to do."

"No. It's not about him. I wanted to ask you something."

What a relief.

"Where did you..." She hesitated. The somberness in Grace's voice sent warning signals off in Avery's head. "When did you decide that you don't want marry a man like him?"

"So this is about Liam?"

"No, it's not. Put him out of your head. This is something I want to know."

This was typical Grace. Always acting like a concerned mother. Avery shrugged. "I don't know. It's just something that I've always felt strongly about."

"I feel strongly about not wearing liquid base, but I'm not going to boycott the makeup aisle."

"I'm not boycotting the entire aisle, just certain brands."

"Why?"

"Why does it matter?"

Another pause. This one long enough for Avery to escape to her room, jump into bed, and slip out of her responsibilities. But she stayed put.

"I think I misled you with Nathan's death."

Avery jerked her focus to her sister's face. Grace never talked about Nathan. Maybe twice since the day he'd passed. "What do you mean misled me?"

"If I had it to do all over again, I still would have picked him, married him."

"So?" Avery was confused.

"Even if it meant losing him again."

"You would?" Avery's lungs tightened.

"Yes." Grace's head bobbed up and down. "Because my love for him was until death do us part. But my love for God is even greater."

"What does that mean?"

"On my wedding day, when I said my vows to Nathan, I also vowed everything I had to God. And if He wanted to take it from me, then I would still love Him."

Avery let her gaze linger. "And did you?"

Grace drew in a shallow breath. "For a while I didn't know how to. But eventually, yes. When I gave my life to Him, I did so with the understanding that everything I need is in Him. And that's where I found my healing."

Grace had never shared this side of her grief with Avery. Now, hearing it aloud, made things real again. As if Nathan had just been taken from them.

"It's been almost ten years, Avery. It's not easy. But it's life. The sorrow never went away for me, but I've learned to make due. You have to. I've discovered how to enjoy the small things that I didn't notice before. I've found myself more thankful for things in general. You learn to appreciate life in a new way. I'll never be the same as I was before Nathan died, I've realized that. But I *have* healed.

"When we lose someone like that, someone who feels like our other half, we can make the choice to hold on to that pain and depression, and we can let ourselves fall apart. Or we can take time to let the hurt go and keep living life. The way God meant for us to."

Avery rubbed the back of her hand against her nose.

"I loved Nathan with everything inside of me. And he'll always claim a piece of my heart. But I've moved on. In fact," Grace let out a shaky laugh. "I'm sorta seeing someone."

Avery's jaw dropped. "You are?"

Grace looked down at her hands. "It's not really serious—yet. We're good friends, but I like him a lot. And I think he likes me, too."

For some reason, Avery's shoulders felt light. As if some kind of weight had been taken from them. "Do I know him?"

"It's Nathan's best friend. Jack."

Avery's spirits fell. "He's a firefighter, too."

"I know." Grace nodded emphatically. "Which is why I told you. Because I can't live in fear of losing the people I love. And neither can you."

"Grace," Avery moaned, unsure if she wanted to cry or put up a fight.

"Don't try to give me a long list of reasons why I shouldn't fall in love with Jack. Because it won't work with me. I want you to see that I can go on living even when tragedy strikes. And so can you."

Avery looked away.

"Letting Nathan go was the worst thing I ever had to do, especially when I lost the baby. But I've healed and I don't want to hold on to that sorrow anymore."

Grace pressed her hands against her heart, her voice tearing. "I love my King Jesus so much that I want to show Him that nothing comes between Him and me. Not even my husband's death. And it's not because I know He holds Nathan and our baby right now. It's because I want Him to hold me. Everyday. For eternity. Me and Him. So I make it a point to praise Him even when I want to blame Him."

Avery rubbed her neck where her throat burned.

"The bottom line is that I'm no longer grieving over Nathan. And I think it's okay that you stop grieving over him, too."

Avery turned her head away. A tear trickled down her cheek, away from Grace's view.

She hadn't even realized it. She was mourning over Nathan. And it had been ten years.

Grace never talked about him. How was she supposed to know her sister had been healed? For all she knew she was living with a broken widow.

But that wasn't true.

She, too, could stop holding onto the reminder that Nathan was no longer with them. She could get on with her life. She was free. Free to live. Free to laugh. Free to love.

Avery quickly swiped away the tear. "I get what you're saying, Grace. And I promise you I'll take it to heart. But if you think this is going to change things with Liam, then you're wrong."

"Am I?"

"I won't make the same mistake twice."

"Your only mistake is walking away from him." The sobriety in Grace's eyes made Avery's skin crawl.

CHAPTER SEVENTEEN

Liam initially had lunch on his mind, but a chase through Midtown Houston sounded equally appetizing.

It was supposed to be a simple traffic stop after a pickup truck ran through a four-way. Now the two suspects obviously thought they had a better chance on the run.

He flipped on the siren and picked up speed.

"My money's on grand theft," Austin said, his breathing got heavy from the rush of adrenaline. "What do you say, drugs or carjacking?"

Liam ignored his partner's humorous banter. This wasn't the place. But somehow Austin's strength came from his chatter.

"Hold up," Austin yelled as he grabbed the dash.

Liam saw it, too. The passenger door kept flying open. A leg dangled out.

"If he runs, I got him. You follow the driver."

Liam watched with precision, careful not to make a mistake that would take lives.

The vehicle slowed enough for a male to fall out, roll into the ditch, and bounce back to his feet.

Liam hit the brakes and Austin bailed out and

followed the guy's tracks. The truck's tires squealed as they tore off. Liam stayed on their tail. Red and blue lights in his rearview told Liam backup wasn't far.

He prayed this guy would pull over. A major highway was coming up and noon may as well be rush hour.

His heart drummed heavy against his bulletproof vest. His hands tensed around the steering wheel as he swerved through traffic.

They merged onto the highway with Liam close. Cars honked as the pickup veered in and out of traffic. He sideswiped a car that was parallel parked and knocked off the mirror.

The second cruiser overtook Liam and attempted to spin the vehicle to a stop by ramming into back side of the truck bed. The truck swerved but regained control and screeched off. A cloud of smoke accumulated around the tires. The cruiser lost speed and Liam regained the lead.

He tried the pit maneuver again, this time making a little more progress. The truck lost control and came to a tire-burning halt.

Before Liam had time to slow down a minivan turned in front of him. He spun the wheel hard to the right, but lost traction. His arms flexed against the jerking wheel as his car jumped the curve and plummeted into the ditch. It lurched back toward the road and clipped a culvert. His cruiser went airborne and flipped.

Once…twice…three times…

CHAPTER EIGHTEEN

Avery glanced down at the number on her ticket and then at the rows of seats. She followed Carol and attempted to match the row number.

"Here it is." Carol gestured to the seat Branson had just passed.

A line of three unappealing plane seats awaited them, empty.

Branson slid each of their carry-ons in the compartment above. Avery took the window seat. She needed something to keep her mind off...things.

Carol eased into the middle seat with a sleeping Jeremy cradled in her arms and took the diaper bag from Branson. "I'm relieved. I was sure he was going to spend the entire flight fussy."

"If he starts to wake up you just give him to his Aunt Avery." Avery tapped his soft little nose.

"Avery?" Carol's perfectly manicured eyebrows drew together in the middle. "Are you sure you want to do this?"

"Do I really have a choice? My bedroom is already halfway to Rome."

Carol snickered and laid her head back on the seat. "I

haven't gotten any sleep in months."

The girl on the loud speaker started to give the flight takeoff instructions, including a warning for all electronics.

Avery reached into her back pocket for her phone. "Jeremy's only three weeks old."

Carol gave her a sidelong glance. "It feels like months."

As Avery touched the power button, her phone began to ring. She didn't recognize the number, but she answered anyway. "Hello?"

"Is this Avery Sanders?" An unfamiliar male voice sounded grave.

Carol elbowed her. "You're not supposed to be on the phone."

"This is she."

He cleared his throat and inhaled deeply. "Ma'am, my name is Austin Brooks. I'm a police officer and Liam Reed is my partner."

"Okay?"

"He, uh," the officer's voice faltered, pushing Avery to the edge of her seat. "He's been involved in a car accident."

The breath left her.

"I thought I should let you know. Since you and, uh, Liam were—"

"How is he?"

The silence all but answered her question. "He's not good."

"Where—" The impulse to swallow cut her question in half. "Where is he?"

"Adams Medical Center."

She hung up and grabbed her purse.

"What's wrong?" Carol asked.

"It's Liam." Her throat ached. "He's been in an accident." She sidestepped Carol and Branson. "Go without me."

The plane's doors had yet to close. Avery left the

airport and hailed a taxi. When one finally stopped she slid into the sticky leather seat and tossed a hundred dollar bill toward the driver.

"Adams Medical Center. Fast. Please."

He drove slower than she wanted. Nearly rush hour, she couldn't argue with him. She bounced her legs, pushed a strand of hair out of her face, and watched the road ahead.

She couldn't think straight. Everything seemed blurry. Like a dream.

They were close to the hospital when the traffic backed up and they were forced to a complete stop behind a BMW.

"Please, keep going."

"I cannot. There are too many cars." The driver looked at her through the rearview mirror.

She wanted to cry from sheer agony.

"The hospital is around that corner, miss. Two blocks." He pointed over the traffic.

Avery got out of the car and ran with everything she had. Past the drove of honking cars and onto the sidewalk where she broke through a crowd of people. The hospital sign came into view and she crossed another lane of traffic to get to the parking lot.

Please, God, don't let it be too late. She ran. The wind stung her already burning eyes.

Save him. God, help him. She ran. Her arms ached, her legs had gone numb.

Don't let him die. She ran. Her lungs seared.

The glass doors of the ER slid open as she approached. The officer she'd seen standing in front of the youth center met her in the waiting room.

"Where is he?"

"He's in surgery."

"I need to see him."

"You will."

She walked past him toward the desk. "Where is he?"

A nurse came out of nowhere and placed her hands gently on Avery's shoulders. "Ma'am. Please."

"I need to see him." The tears fell but she couldn't feel them.

Another nurse ran down the hall towards them. And another.

"Where is he?" She was turning around in circles, searching for someone that could answer her.

"Avery." Dorinda ran toward her, dressed in scrubs. "He's in ICU. He's still alive."

Avery grabbed Dorinda's arms and squeezed hard, searching for hope she couldn't find. "I need to see him."

"I know, baby. Listen to me. He needs you to be strong right now. Okay?" Dorinda looked into her eyes and didn't relent until Avery mimicked her nod. "Right now, you need to keep calm. I can't let you go back to intensive care like this. Okay?"

Avery breathed deep and forced herself to calm. She had to see him.

Dorinda led Avery and Officer Brooks down a long hallway to an elevator. The seconds seemed like years. The scent of cleaning supplies and sickness was unbearable. Avery used the handrails to brace herself.

"Only family can visit, but since Liam doesn't have any immediate family I trust you to be there for him." Dorinda looked between Avery and the officer.

Avery focused on one breath at a time. A bell rang out and the elevator came to a stop. She followed Dorinda around the corner and to a door where she stopped.

She looked at Avery, her eyes watery. "You can't get hysterical."

Avery nodded quickly.

She opened the door. The smell of disinfectant and latex knocked Avery back. The room was dark and cold.

Liam lay on the bed, unresponsive. The low-pitched beep of the heart monitor gave the only sign of life. There were more screens around him than she cared to count.

Wires, tubes, and pumps were everywhere. She stepped inside and her stomach turned.

He was unrecognizable.

He wasn't Liam.

He was just a body.

Fresh cuts covered his swollen face. Tubes funneled through his mouth, down his throat. Bandages peeked from beneath the gown over his shoulders. A cast covered his left arm. A thick white sheet lay over the rest of him.

"He's on life support," Dorinda whispered.

Liam blurred through the tears. Avery clapped her hand over her mouth to hold back a wail.

"Dorinda." A man wearing a white jacket stood in the doorway.

Dorinda grabbed hold of Avery's elbow and guided her out of the room, Officer Brooks followed. In the hallway, lit with the evening sunlight, the doctor shook Avery's trembling hand.

"Dr. Gary Watson. I'm Officer Reed's physician."

"Is he—Will he be all right?" Avery nearly begged.

"Ma'am, you've got to understand the extent of his injuries. Mr. Reed has been through a horrific accident. At this point he's lucky to be alive." Dr. Watson adjusted the stethoscope hanging over his neck

"But he will be okay?"

The doctor pressed his lips firmly together and hesitated. "He has a collapsed lung. Internal bleeding. Broken bones. He's in a coma. I would like to be direct with you in the fact that we're only giving him a ten percent chance of survival."

"Please don't tell me that." Bile rose in the back of Avery's throat. She turned around and followed the hallway back to the elevator.

"Avery," Dorinda called.

She kept pressing the button but the doors wouldn't open. She couldn't see anything. She left the elevator and went to the exit at the end of the hall. She shoved the door open and rushed into the nauseating echo of the stairwell.

She only made it to the first platform and fell against the white, cinderblock wall.

"Why?" she cried. "Why him, Lord?"

Her darkest nightmare was staring her in the eyes with no sign of mercy.

She fell to her knees. "Why would You do this to him?"

Her throat felt raw, her chest heaved. But she mustered the energy to look upward into the towering room. "You knew I would love him. And You would take him from me now?" She sucked in a harsh breath. "How could You do this to me, God? How could You bring me here?"

Everything she'd strived to avoid had followed her.

In the women's restroom where she had tossed the contents of her stomach, Avery pulled her hair into a ponytail and washed her face.

She made her way down the hall and stopped at the door to Liam's room. Her legs quivered. Her lungs hurt. Everything hurt.

A nurse stood beside Liam. She gave Avery a smile over her shoulder and looked back at her clipboard. "Are you Avery?"

"Yeah," she said, her voice nearly gone.

"I'm Tara." She turned around and dropped the clipboard at the foot of the bed. "It's nice to meet you."

Avery couldn't think. Her eyes stayed on the man that lay on the bed.

"If you need anything just hit that button over there." She gestured, but Avery didn't follow. "I'll be down the hall."

When the girl left, Avery walked over to the window on the opposite side of the room and pushed the blinds back. What sunshine was left spilled in. She could see him better.

She braved closer to the bedside and searched his face.

It was him.

She didn't want it to be him. Maybe a case of mistaken identity. Maybe a nightmare. She'd prefer either to this miserable reality.

He had a massive gash on his chin, stretching along his jaw, covered in stitches. She'd give anything to see his blue eyes again and that brown blemish that had become so familiar to her. A drop of dried blood stained on the tip of his ear, leading her to images of the crash that she didn't want to see. She forced her thoughts to his hair.

Mussed and somewhat damp it laid forward over his forehead. She was afraid to touch him. Afraid that if she did the truth of the situation would revive her tears. Although there were no tears left to give.

She lifted her hand until it hovered over his face. Then she pressed her fingers into the short, dark brown locks. She slowly smoothed them back, piece by piece, until he started to look a bit more like the man she had fallen in love with.

He belonged to her.

"I'm going to take care of you, Liam. Every day until you get better. I won't leave. I'll be here."

She let her fingers trace the edge of his face ever so lightly, down to his jaw, along the stitches. She thought to pray, but prayers were hard to come by when she was praying to Someone who had brought her to this.

She would save her breath until Liam opened his eyes, then she'd tell him how much she loved him.

"Avery?" Carol stood in the doorway, Branson behind her. "Can we come in?"

She went to her sister and hugged her tight.

"How is he?"

Avery pulled away and took in a deep breath. She had to be strong. For Liam. "He, uh, he's on life support."

Branson stepped around his wife and pulled Avery into a hug, being careful not to crush Jeremy bundled in his father's arms. "I'm so sorry, honey." He kissed her forehead. "What can we do?"

"Just wait." She'd gone over it a million times in her head. The answer was simply wait. "That's all we can do."

"And pray," Carol added, searching Avery's face.

She ignored the penetrating look. "He has internal bleeding, broken bones, a collapsed lung."

Carol sucked in a gasp. "Has he woken at all?"

Avery shook her head. "He's in a coma."

Carol's eyebrows bunched, a tear fell from her lashes. Branson pulled his wife close. "I'm so sorry, Avery."

Everything Avery had ever dreamt about lay on that bed, battered and on the edge of death.

She couldn't believe she'd let her fears stop her from loving him. She'd pushed him away and now, as he slept as still as a corpse, she couldn't remember why.

"I'm going to stay here with him until he wakes up."

"Do they know when that'll be?" Carol pulled a tissue from her purse.

"No." She chewed on her cheek.

Silence filled the room. There wasn't much to be said. But then again waiting felt like drowning.

"You missed your flight," Avery said.

Carol wiped her nose. "That's a small concern right now."

She bit her lip and nodded.

"As we were coming up, the waiting room was full of officers who want to see him. I think some of them will be up in a bit."

"That's fine."

"I'll call Grace and get her to pack a bag for you and

we'll bring it back later."

"Thanks."

Carol gave her another hug. "You'll be okay?"

"I will." She gave Branson a hug and turned back to Liam. "I'm right where I need to be."

Carol paused at the door. "We'll bring your Bible by, too."

Avery pulled in a long breath. "Leave it."

CHAPTER NINETEEN

The next morning, Avery sat back in the red upholstered hospital chair and watched a police officer walk out the door.

Dorinda stepped in and went to Liam's side.

"What number was he?" Avery asked.

"Four. There should be one more this evening."

It felt as if she'd done nothing but meet the entire police force. She'd left the hospital once only to take a walk in the garden beside the parking lot. And then she returned to Liam's side helping the nurses with what she could.

Avery leaned forward and ran her fingers through his hair. "Dorinda?"

"Huh?" She looked up.

"Please tell me he's doing better."

Dorinda's shoulders fell. "He's not, honey."

Avery lowered her head until it was propped against her hand.

"The doctor will be in shortly."

Footsteps told her Dorinda had left.

She sat there for what felt like forever. Just like last night. When she heard the doctor's voice outside the door, she stood to greet him.

He didn't step inside. He stood in the hallway, talking with another man. Liam's name echoed into the room. Caught off guard, she watched the door and when the doctor didn't come in, she left Liam's side and stepped into the hall.

Dr. Watson stopped talking and looked at Avery, his mouth slack.

"What's this about?" Avery asked. She had a right to know.

"Miss Sanders, this is Kevin Romano. Mr. Romano, Avery Sanders, Mr. Reed's significant other," Dr. Watson said. "This is Mr. Reed's Agent of the Court."

Avery didn't like the sound of that. "What—what does that mean?"

Dr. Watson shifted his stance and tucked a clipboard at his side. "Mr. Reed signed an advance directive in place of his next of kin, should a situation such as this come up."

Avery turned her focus to the man. "What are you supposed to do?"

"Well, ma'am, given that Mr. Reed is on life support and cannot make decisions for himself, the judgment becomes mine."

Avery's spine straightened. "What judgment?"

The doctor and the lawyer looked at one another and back at her. "Ma'am, I'm going to be frank with you. I've reviewed Mr. Reed's medical circumstances and I've gone over them with Dr. Watson. The bottom line is that, at this point in the treatment, Mr. Reed's life support has become futile. Therefore, I'm having it discontinued."

"Wait. What?" She would give him one chance to tell her she'd misheard him.

In her peripheral vision, she saw Dorinda come around the corner with JJ at her side. They stopped quickly.

"We're pulling the plug, Miss Sanders."

"Will he wake up?" She knew the answer.

"There's a small chance he may continue to breathe on his own, but in all honesty that doesn't seem probable."

She felt like the world caved in on her. "Then why would you pull the plug?"

"Like I said, ma'am. The treatment has become futile."

"I heard you the first time, but that doesn't change the fact that he may die."

They were silent.

"You'll let him die?"

"We'll leave that to the Almighty."

"No." Her knees went weak again. "No. Please wait. I'm begging you."

"Waiting will not do any good. If he's going to live then he'll do it today as well as he will tomorrow."

"But I can't lose him today." She broke again. Would the tears ever stop?

The lawyer pulled in an exasperated breath and huffed it out. "Out of my sympathy for you, I'll make the exception for twenty-four hours. But that's all he has. Then the doctor has my order to end all treatments at once. If he lives then I give him the command to take every measure possible to save Mr. Reed's life as per his wishes." He lifted the briefcase in his hand and walked away.

Dr. Watson stayed. He sighed and lowered his gaze to her, his forehead wrinkled. "I'm sorry, Avery."

"Do whatever you can to save him," she demanded, her heart relieved, but still breaking.

"We're not doing any less. It all comes down to whether or not it's his time."

She bit down hard. That wasn't the final answer. She wasn't going to let him go as easily as the doctor could.

He followed the lawyer's path around the corner and out of sight.

Avery turned her focus to JJ. He stared at her, his

eyebrows arched, as if he were holding back tears. His shoulders began to shake. Dorinda spun him around, looked into his face, and her jaw dropped. "Come here, baby."

Dorinda guided him down the hallway, toward the window where the sun illuminated their figures into silhouettes. He sat back on a bench and Dorinda kneeled in front of him.

"Justin, you are going to be strong for Officer Reed. Do you hear me?"

His head bobbed up and down and he wiped his nose with his arm. "Is he going to die?"

"We're not going to worry about that right now."

He sniffed, his voice broken. "Mawmaw?"

"What, honey?"

"Can we pray for Officer Reed?"

Dorinda hesitated. Her shoulders shook once. Then twice as she began to cry. She smiled at her grandson. "Of course, we can pray for him."

They bowed their heads together and JJ spoke to God like he was talking to a friend.

Avery pressed her fingers against her cheek to wipe away an errant tear. She walked inside the hospital room, to the chair that she'd called home for days, and reached into her suitcase.

She pulled out the Bible she'd told Carol not to bring.

The glass doors parted for Avery and she stepped outside. She squinted against the glare of the sunset. Her throat burned. She mindlessly put one foot in front of the other, following the concrete path.

It didn't make sense to her that God would reveal

Himself as a cruel master. That wasn't the Savior she'd grown to know. But the pain that surrounded her made her want to believe that He was. He'd taken Nathan from them. And now, after she'd spent years striving to avoid the same tragedy, He was taking Liam, too.

Tiny white flowers covered the archway that led to the hospital garden. There wasn't much privacy here. A line of traffic waited on the other side of the vine-covered fence.

She sat down at a picnic table and flipped her Bible open to the first passage in the book of Psalms. Her bracelet brushed the tabletop. She craved peace but the words were lost on her. They seemed empty and meaningless. Nothing she could apply to her situation. Nothing to give her hope.

"Lord, I don't know what to do." Was He still here at this point? Did He even care about her?

She pressed her fingers against her forehead. It felt like she'd had this headache forever. She couldn't remember the last time she felt normal. She couldn't remember what life felt like before all of this. And it'd only been two days.

She slid her legs from under the table and walked toward a tree. Her charm bracelet slipped from her wrist and landed in the dirt. She picked it up and tried to put it back on, but she couldn't see the clasp through the tears.

"Why would You bring me here?" She gripped the bracelet in her fist. "Why would You bring Liam here? He doesn't deserve this."

Silence. Not that she'd expected a reply.

Avery stubbornly dried her tears and turned back to her bracelet. She worked her shaking fingers to hook the clasp back in place. Then she instinctively grabbed the charm that felt soft to the touch and caught a glimpse of the word trust.

Nothing could be trusted. Not life. Not this world. Not even God.

She could no longer trust Him with her life or with her future.

She never did.

The breath left her lungs and she couldn't get it back. As if a ton of bricks landed on her midsection when she realized...

She never trusted God to begin with.

Not when it came to Liam.

The One she'd claimed to believe in had answered a lifetime of prayers. He'd sent her the perfect man and she'd shut Liam out long before she'd ever met him.

Nathan's death.

She'd taken her trust out of Jesus and placed it in her own ability to choose the right companion. She'd failed more times than she knew. And she'd failed again when this man had walked into her life.

She hadn't trusted God's judgment to provide her with a hope and a future. She'd trusted herself. She still did, which is why she'd abandoned any thought of God as soon as she saw Liam in that hospital bed.

"No." She bent over at the waist when a pain shot through the pit of her stomach.

That couldn't be true. Surely somewhere she trusted God with her future, with Liam's future.

But she didn't. In the crevices of her mind all she could hear were her own straightforward opinions about never dating a man who would sacrifice his life for his job.

Even that didn't work.

And she had blamed God for it.

She backed up until her legs touched the bench and sat, her back to her Bible. She let her face fall against her hands. "What have I done?"

She'd been wrong all along. Grace was right. She could feel the truth ringing in her sister's words.

Grace had worn the shoes Avery wore now. She'd been down this road and she'd given Avery the best advice she could get. But Avery had paid it no mind. She thought she could do the best for herself. And this was where she'd landed with a heartache she couldn't heal and a hundred miles away from her faith.

"Jesus," she breathed. "I'm sorry. I was naive to think I could do this myself. I can't believe how far I took this. Forgive me."

She wiped away a tear, the wind blowing her hair across her bowed face. "I trust in You. My faith is in You. I don't want to do it like this anymore. My way doesn't work." Clearly.

But there was more. She knew there was more. And it nearly ripped her heart out of her chest to admit it.

"And, Lord I..." She struggled to catch her breath. "Lord. I promise You that no matter what happens to Liam, I'll love You. You'll still be my King. No matter what happens."

She knew if she said it then she had to uphold it. The day was fast approaching...

Once the ache in her chest lessened, she turned around and looked at her Bible. The wind had turned the pages back a chapter. Job.

He was the guy that lost it all. Everything he lived for had been taken from him and still he praised God. Even despite his wife's requests to curse God and die.

And there Avery sat, blaming God for Liam's condition while she was the very one who'd pushed him away. She flipped her Bible closed and left the garden.

Her heart felt renewed, heavy with a different kind of weight.

But she still prayed. "Lord, please don't take him from me."

CHAPTER TWENTY

Avery stood at Liam's bedside, a stack of papers in hand. Her eyes roved over the words but they were gibberish to her.

Twenty-four hours, six lawyers, and no answers.

There was nothing she could do.

They all told her the same thing. Liam's life was in the hands of his lawyer. A few of them had looked over Liam's paperwork, but in the end they all pushed it back across the desk, shaking their heads.

She wasn't going to let it end this way. She wanted control over Liam's life support.

Past the papers she looked at his face. The cuts remained the same. His facial hair was starting to show. But he was still as lifeless as he'd been three days ago.

"Avery?" Grace said, standing against the wall on the other side of the room.

"Yeah?" She looked up.

"Are you all right?"

No. "Of course."

Grace's eyebrows arched in the middle. Holding Jeremy, Carol sat beside her in the only chair. "I wish Branson would hurry."

Avery knew why, but she didn't want to face it. Grace and Carol wanted everyone to be there for Avery when they...

Avery's breathing turned quick and shallow.

Her parents were getting on a flight from Georgia tomorrow but she needed their strength and support now.

"Any change?" Austin stood at the door, dressed in his police uniform.

She shook her head.

He stepped into the room. "When are they going to do it?"

Avery got that feeling again, like she was swimming in the ocean with no life vest and no sign of land. She wanted to grab hold of something, to still her shaking limbs, but she was already leaning back against the wall.

"Dorinda guessed it could be a few hours."

His shoulders fell.

"I'm not going to let them." She lifted the papers. She was drowning and no one could hear her scream.

His eyebrows furrowed. "What's that?"

"There are some avenues I'm researching to get control." She was losing control.

"Avery." Compassion reflected in his green eyes.

"You can't just let them kill him. He's your partner. He's your friend, Austin. We've got to do something." She was in over her head and time was running out fast.

"I've already tried. This is the law you're messing with. We can't do anything about that."

She slapped the papers against her thigh. "Fine."

She began reading again. She'd lost her sisters' support and now Austin's. She only had Dorinda on her side.

There were a few things she'd found pertaining to Liam's life support that she could show the doctor. There was a chance he would postpone today until she could find a lawyer to fight her case.

The silence tortured her.

If only someone could speak up, tell her to hold on to hope. Hope she'd given up on a long time ago. In a last ditch effort, she prayed that God would lead the doctor, grant him a change of heart.

Voices echoed down the hall. She stopped reading and rested her eyes on the words.

The voices got closer until she could recognize Dr. Watson's tone. She exhaled, her jaw threatening to quiver. She felt her forehead get warm, ready to break out in a sweat. He appeared in the doorway with a nurse behind him and nodded a greeting to everyone in the room, ending with Avery.

"It's time, Avery."

"Look, Dr. Watson." She took a few steps and met him. "If you would take a moment to look over these. I think you'll find that there's a good chance…" She handed him the papers and watched him pass them to his nurse.

His eyes were distant. "I understand the law fully, Miss Sanders. I've been in this business for close to forty years. Today is the day."

She backed up until she touched Liam's bed. "I can't let you do it."

"I'm going to have to ask everyone to leave the room so the nurses can do their jobs."

Her sisters stood and filed out, Austin stopped near the door.

"Please, don't, doctor. I'm begging you."

"Ma'am. If you don't want to be present, then you'll have to leave."

"Look at him." She raised her voice. "He's going to die. You would let him die?"

"Officer, will you please escort Miss Sanders out?"

Austin stepped forward. "Avery, let's go."

She pressed herself further against the machines, in front of the nurses. "I can't leave him. I'm asking you to reconsider."

"Avery, it's not going to work. We've got to go."

Austin stepped past the doctor and took her arm. "It's over, Avery."

"No, it's not." She tried to pull away.

He tightened his grip. "Please, Avery. Don't fight this."

He tugged her and she fought against him. "Austin, don't."

He wrapped an arm around her midsection and pulled her back.

"They're going to kill him. Please, stop. He's going to die."

Austin dragged her into the hall. She fought harder, jerking away from him, but he held tight.

Tears fell and Avery's voice faded quick. "Don't let them take him from me. I love him. Please, Austin. I'm begging you." She screamed toward the room. "I'm begging you. Please stop. I can't live without him."

She hit Austin on the chest. He held one of her wrists. She started to break loose, but he picked her up and took her further away.

"Please, stop. I'm begging you. Don't take him from me!"

Dorinda stood pressed against the wall, down the hall, watching Avery with tears on her cheeks and a hand over her mouth. Her sisters were on the other side, holding each other, crying.

From where she stood in the hall, Avery watched the nurse remove the IVs and pull the machine away from his bed.

"Please, don't do it."

Then they took the breathing tubes out of his mouth.

"No," she gasped and stopped fighting. Her shoulders fell. She couldn't keep her head up. She couldn't open her eyes. "No."

Austin released his hold on her and she fell to her knees. She fisted the hem of his pants and screamed, "Why would You take him away? How could You do this to me?

Don't You hear me, God? What did I do to You to deserve this?"

The energy left her. The rage, the anger. It sifted away and left behind a longing for a Savior.

"I need You, Jesus." Her heart surrendered. "I worship You still."

She could hear the cry of her sisters grow louder.

"Every day I will bless You. Every day I will seek You. You are a good God and greatly to be praised. The depths of Your understanding are unsearchable."

She sucked in hard. "I will lift You up because of Your great love for me. Father, take me in Your arms and draw me close to Your heart. I don't want to go through this without You. For Your name is mercy and You bring me through the waters when they rise."

She released her grip on Austin. The floor was cold beneath her palms. She wanted to lie down and whisper the name of Jesus.

Austin walked away. Nurses walked around her. Sounds surrounded her but Avery couldn't hear a thing.

Someone touched her back.

"Avery. Honey, they removed the ventilator," Dorinda whispered. "He's breathing on his own."

CHAPTER TWENTY-ONE

Darkness covered the sanctuary except for the flickering candles at the end of the aisle.

Austin Brooks walked slowly between the long, empty rows of pews. He'd noticed this room each time he visited the hospital. Only now he saw reason to step inside and brave the silence, to confront the burden weighing on his chest that made it hard for him to breathe.

His thoughts took him back to Avery, moments ago. The way she fell at his feet in surrender. There was such passion in her voice, dedication. Not to Liam. To God.

She fought to reach Liam. And when Liam was out of reach, she fought for Jesus Christ.

When her prayers for Liam's survival had been answered, Austin had watched Avery and her family kneel around his bed to worship God.

Austin stopped where the pulpit started. He admired the intricate detail of the wooden cross hanging at the back of the hospital chapel. The stained glass windows on each side. The velvet curtains hanging from the ceiling.

He was alone. It made him uncomfortable.

"It's been a while," he said with an echo.

The place was cold. Or was it just him? Austin

shoved his hands in his pockets and exhaled. Trying to make small talk with God sounded redundant to him.

So he said what he came to say. "I want what Avery has."

He'd had it once. A long time ago.

He rubbed a hand over his mouth. "She loves You and she doesn't let anything stand in the way of that. I…I want to be like that."

In his hesitance, he wondered if God even heard him anymore. He'd been quiet for years. Since Austin had walked away from his faith.

"If You're there, God, I want You to know that I want to go back. I want to start loving You again. Like I used to. I…"

Once upon a time Austin had wanted nothing besides God. He remembered times of lifting his hands in praise. Times of rejoicing in who he was and how he was born.

"That was a long time ago," he snapped out.

He felt the bitterness rising.

"It's just that I was supposed to be made in Your image. You said I was fearfully and wonderfully made. But I'm not. You made everybody else in Your image. But not me. Why would Someone who's supposed to love me do that?"

There was no reply.

"Same ol', same ol'," he mumbled.

He didn't leave. He let the venom build up.

"I tried. I really did. So I can't take all the blame, here." He chuckled. "You did this to me. You made me like this. But You really shouldn't care, should you? I mean come on, it's not You they're putting down. No, You wouldn't have any idea how it feels to be treated like you're worthless."

My Son does.

Austin swallowed. Chest tight, his eyes stung. He fisted his hand over his head, like he were bringing down a gavel. And then he let it go.

"Why didn't You do something? Change me? Change them? Why didn't You step in on my behalf? I needed You and You didn't do anything."

He resisted the urge to pick up something and throw it. "Do You know the things they said to me? Do You know what they did to me? I know You made me different than everyone else," he yelled and didn't care who heard him. "But why did I have to be the one to mess everything up? Everything! There's only so much a person can take before you start to wish you were never born."

He broke. Everything inside him broke and pulled him to his knees. He fell against the thick carpet beneath him.

Upstairs, everybody thanked God for Liam's life. But Austin took his for granted. Four years ago, he'd even contemplated ending it.

Guilt like he'd never felt before buried him.

He smothered a tear clinging to his jaw. "I'm sorry, Lord. For everything I've lost. Every time I ignored You. For all the years I spent running from You. If I could go back and change things, I would. But I can't. That's why…"

He leaned forward on his hands. "I need to ask You back into my life. I don't want to do this without You anymore. I'm tired of running."

That was ironic coming from him.

"I'm tired of pretending to be someone else. I just want You back. Nobody else. Nothing else. I want it to be me and You again. I want to love You like I used to and praise You like I used to. I don't care what everybody else thinks or says or does. I only want You."

It would take some time for him to truly not let other people's words bother him, but on this day Austin made a decision to pursue God's will for his life above everything else.

He was back.

CHAPTER TWENTY-TWO

Six times Liam shifted, moaned, or opened his eyes over the course of the night. Each time Avery felt more hopeful that he would pull through. At one point he even mumbled.

Dr. Watson looked over Liam's charts. "It's rare to have a patient come out of a coma with their speech untouched. Most coma victims need speech therapy."

Avery rubbed her fingers across the sleek surface of her trust charm. "So?"

"I suggest you don't get your hopes too high. There may be other injuries that we won't know the extent of until he comes out of the coma."

"Doctor," She whispered, not because she wanted to, but because she was humbled. "I'm just grateful he's alive."

He gave her a gentle smile. "As am I."

Liam shifted lightly beneath the covers, enough to draw their attention.

"Hey, Liam?" The doctor said, placing his fingers against Liam's palm. "Squeeze my hand if you can hear me?"

Avery watched Liam's hand closely, her heartbeat in her throat. She waited for a response, anything to tell her that she hadn't imagined the times he'd moved before.

Ever so slowly, his fingers shifted and touched Dr. Watson's.

"Where?" Liam said, his voice was faded, groggy, unlike him.

"Liam," the doctor spoke a little louder and a little slower. "You're at Adams Medical Center. You're doing fine, son. Stick with us, okay?"

His eyes opened and he stared at Dr. Watson with a wrinkle between his brows. After a minute he turned his head toward Avery.

Tears burned in Avery's eyes and she pressed her palm to her mouth to hold back a wail. But she couldn't stop it. Her heart flowed with love for this man. She touched his rough cheek and leaned close. He stared at her, his eyes bloodshot but no longer swollen.

Did he remember her? Would he forget her now, after everything they'd been through? Would he love her the same as he did before?

His eyes pinched shut and he shifted in his bed. His neck popped as he moved and he groaned.

He opened his eyes again and looked straight at her. At her forehead, her nose, her chin, and back at her eyes. "Didn't...'spect t' see you."

She grinned through the tears. "I'm here. I'm not going anywhere."

A small, solemn, and probably pain-filled smile crossed his mouth before he closed his eyes and returned to sleep.

CHAPTER TWENTY-THREE

Liam's back hurt when they sat him up in his bed for the first time. It felt like someone had shoved a knife in his spine. The fact of the matter was that he was alive. He couldn't complain.

The doctor had just left and Dorinda was getting him settled in. That little movement wore him out, getting situated enough to feel like a human being again.

"I'll be back in to do some exercises with you a little later. For now I want you to rest. Okay?"

"'Kay." He repeated, too worn to nod his head.

She left and the room fell silent.

Liam laid his head back and pulled in a deep breath. From what he could tell his right hand was still functioning but the left was in a cast. His thoughts were hazy but didn't give him concern. What did concern him were his legs.

He opened his eyes and turned his head so he could get a better view of the woman standing beside him, holding his hand in hers.

She was as beautiful as she was the first time they'd met. But she wasn't wearing any makeup. Well, at least not from what he could tell. And she looked like she'd lost a little bit of weight.

"What happened?" He rasped out, still surprised that it was his voice.

"You were in a wreck."

"That makes sense." Although he couldn't remember it.

"A bad one."

He gestured to the arm that wore a cast. "I know."

"I suppose you would." She giggled gently, sounding more feminine and softer than what he could remember.

"They say your car flipped four times," she said.

"Guess I beat my old record."

She was silent, though he couldn't see her. He figured she'd probably been through as much suffering as he had. "Sorry."

"Don't be. Humor is a rare privilege around here lately."

He hummed to let her know he heard her.

"You have a scar...right here." He felt her fingers trace his jawline, from his neck to his chin.

It took every ounce of energy left in him to grab her wrist and press a kiss against her palm. "Why'd you stay?"

"Because." She swallowed. He could see it in her throat. "I love you." She started to tear up. "I'm so sorry for everything that happened, Liam."

"It's not your fault."

"I mean before the wreck." She sat down in the chair beside his bed so that her face was even with his. "Pushing you away like that, I was wrong. I was so wrong. It was my stupid fault for trying to take things into my own hands. And despite it, I almost lost you."

There was regret shimmering in her eyes and in the downward tilt of her lips. She'd matured a lot. Whatever had happened to her while he was out had turned her world upside down.

"You...you do remember that, right?" She blinked a few times. "You remember why I broke up with you?"

He chuckled. "I remember."

Her shoulders relaxed as if she'd been afraid he'd lost his memory.

"You're not scared?"

"Not anymore." She shifted. "I'm done being scared. I'm leaving my fears in God's hands."

"Good." He breathed slowly. "I'm not going to be a cop."

"We'll cross that bridge when we get to it. For now, just rest."

He arched an eyebrow. "We?"

"If you want me here."

"If it were up to me I'd never let you go."

"Good. Then I'll stay." A tear slid down her cheek and clung to her chin.

He finally saw Avery cry. He reached over and wiped the tear away. But he couldn't erase all of her pain.

He wasn't sure she'd want to stay after she found out..."I can't feel my legs."

"I know."

He didn't want to think about it. Didn't want to think about what that might mean.

"I've got some good news," she said.

He hummed.

"Austin gave his heart to Jesus."

He lifted his head. "What?"

"Yeah. While you were out. I guess he decided it was time."

He couldn't believe it. His partner. The one who'd bashed Liam's faith for years, who denied the need for righteousness. He gave his life to the King.

Liam laid is head back and closed his eyes, smiling.

It was all worth it.

CHAPTER TWENTY-FOUR

Liam sat in a wheelchair in the garden outside. He'd been awake for days, but he could barely call life normal again. Avery sat on the bench beside him, letting out her tenth sigh in five minutes.

"Nervous?"

She laughed. "How can you tell?"

"You're transparent, darling."

"Well, don't tell anyone."

"You think I won't meet their standards?"

"Not at all." She traced her finger along the lines of his cast. "They're going to love you."

"You're worried about the diagnosis."

She turned her liquid brown eyes on him.

"If it changes things between us—"

"It won't." She assured him, her jaw set sternly. "I'm more worried for your sake than anything. But it's not going to change the way I feel about you."

"Then you've got nothing to worry about."

She smiled gently and laid her head against his shoulder.

Two people came walking down the sidewalk into the garden. A man, who might have been as tall as Liam had he been standing. And a woman, who looked remarkably similar to Avery.

Liam hated meeting them like this. Hated the feeling of being confined to this chair. He was a cop. He was supposed to stand tall in the name of Texas justice. It stung, but he didn't have a choice.

Avery jumped to her feet. She hugged the man first, then the woman who was tall, but not as tall as Avery.

"So you must be Liam," the man said, shaking hands with Liam.

"Yes, sir."

"Avery has told us so much about you."

His girl smiled at him with a proud glint in her eyes.

"I'm Harrison Sanders. This is my wife, Holly."

Holly's giggle sounded a lot like Avery's. She leaned out and wrapped him in a hug.

"It's nice to meet you both." Liam gave them a curt nod. "I owe my life to your daughter for everything she's done. If it weren't for her, I'd be sitting up in the room by myself, waiting for something good to come along."

"You'd be just as well without me." Avery quirked an eyebrow and touched his shoulder.

"My heart would be worse off."

She smiled in that way of hers that told him he caught her off guard.

Her mother gasped. "I cannot believe it. That's so sweet. How about we go out to lunch? We rented an accessible van so you'll be more comfortable, Liam."

"Oh, Mom. Liam has to meet with the specialist before we leave."

"All right. We'll wait right here. Once you two are ready, we'll head out."

Liam didn't feel like making a public appearance. But for Avery's sake he would brave it.

Avery pushed him back into the hospital. "Are you ready?"

He breathed deep. "Are you?"

"Of course." But she wouldn't look at him.

He'd already asked himself the question a hundred times. Would she still love him if he never walked again? He'd even asked her, given her the option to leave, but she proved a stubborn woman.

He liked that about her.

If she didn't love him in the same way, he couldn't expect her to stay. But then he wondered if there was another angle she was worried about. One that would destroy them more deeply than useless legs.

They got to the room and Avery parked Liam near the bed while she waited by the door.

"Good morning." The orthopedic surgeon stepped inside. "How are we today?"

"Getting better every day." Liam assured him.

"That's good news." He kneeled down in front of Liam's wheelchair and started working with his legs. "How's that?"

Liam nodded. "I can feel it."

"That's an improvement."

He pressed a tool to the bottom of his foot. Liam flinched.

"We've done enough tests on you this week that you ought to feel like you're back in college." The doctor's joke fell flat. "In my professional opinion, I see a good chance that you'll walk again. I'd give it about six months to a year of physical therapy and some hard work. The scans came back with positive results, so I'm very optimistic about your future."

"And what about my job?"

The doctor quickly looked at him. "That's a bit ambitious, isn't it?"

"I just want your opinion."

"I won't give you any promises because this is something we'll have to take one day at a time. But I've seen patients with a worse prognosis do more. So I can't necessarily rule out the possibility that you'll return to the force. However, the likeliness wouldn't come any time soon. Like I said. We'll take this one day at a time."

Liam didn't realize he was holding his breath until those words were spoken.

"That's great news, doctor."

"It's no trouble. I'll have the nurse set you up a schedule with physical therapy."

As the doctor moved away, Avery came into view on the other side of the room. She sat in a chair, her elbows on her knees, her head bowed.

"You didn't want me to walk."

Her head jerked up, her eyes wide, and she stood. "Liam, do *not* say that. Of course I want you to walk."

"But you didn't want me to be a cop again."

She slowly sat back down.

He was right.

"That's always going to be a fear. Hoping that you don't get hurt again." She cleared her throat. "But it's my job to leave that fear in God's hands. To trust His will no matter what happens. And I'll make it a point to spend all of my time loving who you are and what you do instead of being scared of it." A tear fell from her lashes.

His heart skipped a beat. "This isn't going to be easy."

"It's all going to work out."

"You'll be able to get through it?"

"*We'll* be able to get through it."

Liam watched her closely. "Do you think you could be happy being a cop's wife?"

After a quiet moment, Avery lifted her head with a grin. "I do."

EPILOGUE
A Year and a Half Later

Deep Waters Coffee House

Avery Reed stood in the middle of the empty coffee shop, admiring the sign that hung behind the counter. Hands on her hips, she thought back to the moment she and Liam had chosen the name six months ago.

"Isn't it amazing when you think about everything God has brought us through," he'd said. "And now you own a coffee shop."

"Kind of like the scripture says…" She'd hugged his arm tighter. "He'll be with us when we pass through the water and the rivers won't overtake us. It's like we were in deep water, but we didn't drown. He was with us. He was always with us."

"Deep waters?" Liam's mouth had curved in consideration. "Deep Waters Coffee. I sorta like it."

"Deep Waters Coffee House," she'd added. "I like it, too."

After a year of planning and praying, she was finally here. Avery never dreamed that she would open her own coffee shop, until she'd resigned her future to God's will. Since that day her heart had grown abundant with hopes and aspirations she'd never considered.

Avery's maxi dress swayed as she waddled up to the counter where the calendar lay sprawled open with notes scribbled across this month and the next. She picked up a pen and pulled the top off with her teeth.

She wrote the words "Grand Opening" beside Friday for the fifth time, in a different color. A grin spread across her face, although it was still four days away. She tapped today's date with the end of the pen, where the words "Happy Anniversary" were written.

A year ago today she'd married the love of her life.

Avery remembered the day Liam proposed. Six weeks after he walked away from his wheelchair, Liam had taken her to the Williams Tower Waterfall and asked her to be his wife. Overjoyed, she'd said yes and they set a quick wedding date. Now they were celebrating a year of married life.

Avery laid a hand against her rounded midsection.

It wouldn't be long before they welcomed a new Reed into the world. Her doctor estimated about two weeks left. They'd asked him not to reveal the gender until the birth so they could enjoy the surprise.

Someone came through the entrance door behind her and Avery's heart skipped a beat as it did often when he was near.

Liam's arms wrapped around her and she leaned back against his chest.

"How's my baby and its momma doing?" He pressed a kiss to her neck.

"They're hungry. A girl could starve waiting on you." She turned around in his embrace and wrapped her arms around his neck. She loved the way he looked in his black, long-sleeve uniform. His hair a mess after taking off his hat. "How was your first day back?"

He shrugged. "They got me doing a lot of deskwork.

I expected as much. But I'm ready to get back in the field."

"I know you are." She smiled as she kissed him deeply. As if it were the first time.

He pulled away and rested his head against hers. "I love you so much."

"I love you, too," she whispered.

"You ready to go?"

She nodded.

"Let me go wash up real quick." He stepped into the customer bathroom off the café.

Avery sighed, her waist still tingling where his hands had rested. There were no words she could use to thank God for the gifts he had given her. All she could do was rest in His grace.

All of the sudden, the room seemed to spin. As if something had shifted in the air around her. She pressed her palm against her stomach and felt the baby move. She'd been having cramps all week but the doctor said she might have false labor pains further into the pregnancy.

Now, she wasn't so sure they were false.

Liam stepped out of the bathroom, drying his hands with a rag. "I talked to Austin earlier."

A sharp pain cut down her spine, causing her to suck in a hard breath.

Liam walked past her and tossed the rag on the counter. "He said he's thinking about leaving the police force. Said God is putting something different on his heart."

She swallowed and grabbed the back of the nearest chair.

"Did you spill something?" Liam asked, looking at the floor beneath his shoes.

"My water broke."

Liam's mouth dropped open, his eyes widened. "Your water? Wait! What—what—should I call nine-one-one?"

"Liam, you *are* nine-one-one." Avery gritted her teeth. "I thought I was having Braxton Hicks Contractions, but—" The next pain made her lose all train of thought. She screamed so loud it even startled her.

She felt Liam grab her hand and wrap an arm around her back. One step in front of the other was all she could focus on until they were outside and the pain eased up.

"Lock the door," She said between breaths.

"Avery, we don't have—"

"Just lock it. I don't want to get robbed before the opening."

Liam growled as he pulled out his keys, went back to the door, and did as she asked.

Another pain came with another blood-curdling scream and he was back at her side in a heartbeat. She squeezed his finger so hard she was sure they were broken.

He opened the door but she couldn't step up inside. She pushed her head against his chest and started to cry. "Babe, I can't do this."

"You don't have a choice." He pushed her toward the truck, but she couldn't move.

"It hurts."

"I need you to get in the truck, baby."

The contractions paused long enough for her to get in. She wanted to put her feet against the dash, but resisted the urge. She grabbed the handle over the door and squeezed like it depended on her life. Sweat had already broken out across her forehead.

Seconds felt like hours as Liam started the truck and pulled away from their coffee shop. Traffic was at its worst when Avery realized the baby wasn't going to wait. There was too much pressure on her cervix. "Liam?"

"I'm going as fast as I can, honey." He hit the horn and mumbled under his breath, "Wish I had my cruiser."

"Liam?"

She could see alarm flash through his eyes. "What's wrong?"

"The baby's coming." She grabbed his sleeve and pulled so tight the button popped off the cuff. "Right now!"

Liam inhaled and turned into the next parking lot.

"Wait! The hospital."

He didn't reply. Instead, he picked up his cell phone and came around to her side of the truck with it pressed between his ear and his shoulder. "This is Officer Liam Reed."

He helped her out of the passenger seat at the wrong time. Another pain gripped her midsection and she dug her nails into his arm.

Liam yelled. "Aaahh! We need an ambulance in front of Righteous Hope Baptist Church. My wife is in labor and—"

Avery wailed as she slid into the backseat and laid down.

"—oh, man." Liam's voice grew thick. "The baby's head is out."

"Liam, it's coming. The baby!" She howled.

He hung up and crawled into the seat between her feet.

"What are you doing?" She grabbed the headrest and pulled her back against the door, her face wet with tears and sweat.

"We're having a baby." He rolled his sleeves up, like a cowboy getting ready to deliver a calf.

"Have you ever delivered a baby before?" Her voice was getting weaker.

He glanced up at her with a half-smile. "Let's pretend like I have."

"This isn't right." Her breathing turned into wheezing. "It's too fast, Liam. Carol's baby didn't come this fast. What's wrong?"

"Nothing's wrong. Some babies just come quicker than others. I think it's called prasic—or precit—"

"Precipitous labor." She spouted out.

"Yeah. That."

She screamed again and pushed as hard as she could.

"Breathe," Liam reminded her.

"I can't breathe!" She scolded him and pinched her eyes closed. "Oh! It hurts so bad."

"You're doing good, Avery."

"Liam, please stop talking." She begged. But she wanted to hear his voice, too.

"One more push, honey. You can do this."

She pushed again. Harder and longer this time. Sudden relief flooded her body.

When she sucked in, she heard the most precious sound on the face of the earth. A sound she'd dreamed about for nine months.

She heard her baby cry.

She gasped for a deep breath but couldn't find one right away. Her heart banged against her chest like it was trying to break out of her body. She rubbed the sweat away from her eyes and looked up.

Liam held the tiny, bare-skinned baby against his chest. A tear slid down his cheek that he didn't bother to dry. He was beaming, his eyes memorizing their baby's face. Sirens echoed in the distance.

"Avery," his voice was soft and filled with joy. "We have a baby."

She watched her husband in all of his gentleness as he sat in awe of the treasure they'd created. And a precious longing filled her insides with adoration for Liam.

Avery vowed to never stop loving this man.

Coming Soon

The Road to Austin
A Finding Faith Romance: Book 2

Houston, Texas

Austin Brooks had never seen a girl so beautiful.

She was a dream, a drop of innocence in a clouded world. Everything about her was perfect. From her locks of coffee-brown hair to her puckered, bow-shaped lips. And then her eyes, one blue, one brown.

Her name was Hannah and she held Austin's attention like no other female had.

She gave him a toothless smile and he lost himself.

"I wish I could take you with me," he told the infant in his arms.

Liam cleared his throat. "Then you'd have me to deal with."

Austin arched an eyebrow. "Everybody knows uncles are the favorite."

Avery tucked her hands around Liam's arm and held him close. "We'll be sure to remind her often."

Austin took her in once more. For the last time in a while. "It's not fair."

"What's that?" Liam asked.

"She just got here and now I have to leave."

"She'll still be here when you get back."

"That's not the point." Austin hooked a finger beneath her tiny chin.

"You don't have to, you know?" Liam shrugged. "Just say the word and we'll go get your job back at the station."

Austin knew. He'd considered it a hundred times last night while he lay restless in an empty apartment. "This is something I've been praying about for a long time."

"Which is why I know you're making the right decision." Liam slapped him on the shoulder.

Austin somehow managed to lay Hannah in her mother's arms. It wasn't easy. Something in him wished she would have cried and raised her tiny fists for him. But she'd fallen asleep to the motion of his sway.

"Take care of her."

Avery's smile was certain. "We will." She pressed a kiss to his cheek. "Drive careful. See you soon."

He watched her walk the baby into the house.

"So what's next?" Liam asked.

"Austin, Texas. Home." He shrugged. "And then I have no clue."

"You'll call if you need anything?"

"I'll say yeah, but don't hold your breath." Austin shook his partner's hand and pulled him in for a hug. "I'll be back soon."

"We'll be waiting."

Liam backed away as Austin climbed into his truck. He pulled the door closed and leaned out the window. "Take care of those girls for me."

"You have my word."

The diesel roared as he cranked it up. "Later, man."

"Later." Liam nodded and turned toward the house.

Austin shifted the gear into drive as something on his passenger seat caught his attention.

A Bible.

It looked new and certainly didn't belong to him.

He pulled back the cover and found a note on the first page. His eyes repeatedly skimmed the words he recognized as Liam's handwriting:

Austin,

You've become a brother to Avery and I, and that's something we'll never forget. We wish you the best of luck in your journey. Know that you'll constantly be in our prayers. If there's one piece of advice we would give you, it's this; if ever you find yourself at a loss for direction, just put your trust in God and you'll find your way again, it works like a charm.

Liam, Avery, and Hannah

He smiled to himself and turned his focus on the road ahead.

ABOUT THE AUTHOR

Jessica Alyse was born a dreamer. She used to tell stories about a bicycle that traveled to the moon and back. Her imagination has always soared beyond the expectations of reality and has brought her to a career in creative fiction. A storyteller, hopeless romantic, and follower of Christ, she encompasses the appropriate traits to create romantic Christian fiction, embellishing every story with southern charm and wholesome love.

A Louisiana girl with a heart for Texas, when she's not writing, you can typically find her dreaming about the day her books get adapted into movies, practicing for her would-be singing career, or in the event of a football game, cheering for the Green Bay Packers.

Find Jessica's upcoming releases, newsletter sign-up, social media links, and biography on

JessAlyse.com

If you enjoyed reading The Trust Charm,
consider leaving a review on Amazon or Goodreads.
Every review is beneficial to the author as well as
readers, and helps promote books in similar genres.

Thank you.

Made in the USA
Columbia, SC
07 July 2022